英文素養

▷附解析本

寫作攻略

專為 **108 課綱**
量身打造的英文素養寫作寶典

郭慧敏

學歷：美國喬治亞州立大學英語碩士
經歷：新北市立中和高中英語教師

三民書局

U0085556

序

英語 Make Me High 系列的理想在於超越，在於創新。
這是時代的精神，也是我們出版的動力；
這是教育的目的，也是我們進步的執著。

針對英語的全球化與未來的升學趨勢，
我們設計了一系列適合普高、技高學生的英語學習書籍。

面對英語，不會徬徨不再迷惘，學習的心徹底沸騰，
心情好 High！
實戰模擬，掌握先機知己知彼，百戰不殆決勝未來，
分數更 High！

選擇優質的英語學習書籍，才能激發學習的強烈動機；
興趣盎然便不會畏懼艱難，自信心要自己大聲說出來。
本書如良師指引循循善誘，如益友相互鼓勵攜手成長。
展書輕閱，你將發現……
學習英語原來也可以這麼 High！

給讀者的話

　　我喜歡教高中學生英文寫作，一教就是三十年。他們最迫切想知道的不外乎是「如何在有限的時間內寫出 120 字言之有物的英文作文」以及「如何快速掌握大考常見的四類型作文」。這些年來，看過不少學生放棄英文寫作，但也看到許多努力的孩子在老師策略性的引導下，短短幾個月就對寫作充滿信心，因為他們終於懂得如何善用文字表達自己的想法，能將內心的感受化為文字傳遞給他人。

　　在我的課堂上，學生最愛挑戰「二十分鐘輕鬆寫作」，因為可以快速看到自己的成長與蛻變，很有成就感。這讓我產生一股動力，願意花一些時間將這寫作鷹架搭建過程匯集成這本《英文素養寫作攻略》。

　　素養寫作是指透過書寫文字，訓練獨立思考與表達意見等能力。本書透過階段性學習方式，逐步解構寫作概念，引導學生分析題幹、構思整體內容，在有限時間內寫出一篇有邏輯架構的英文短文。此外，綜觀歷屆大考的寫作情境皆與學生的生活情境相關，本書也收錄 Extended Writing Map，訓練學生從範文寫作中延伸練習，結合生活常見議題，培養邏輯思考與創意表達能力。

　　臺灣學生無法避免要面對各種英文檢定測驗和升學考試。不論是出國求學或在國內應徵工作或升遷時，總會有多次準備英文寫作的經驗。無論你過去的經驗多麼的糟糕，我都要鼓勵你：花一些時間讀完這本書，你會看見寫作的脈絡，學會建立系統性思考。

　　素養寫作真的很簡單，掌握書中「2 個寫作三角」和「轉折用語的魔法」，自然會建立自己的寫作模式，突破素養寫作之瓶頸。期待所有需要英文寫作指引的讀者，從此一手掌握自己的思考：我手寫我心！

郭慧敏

Contents

使用説明

Step 1. 解構大考英文作文，掌握考題趨勢脈動。

大考英文作文主要是針對提示中的內容，也就是命題者的要求，逐一回應其問題，並提出自己的看法。從近幾年的作文命題，可以讓我們窺探其中的意味，亦即素養導向情境式評量。由此可觀察出英文作文素養命題的重點，要包含情節 (plot) 與線索 (clue) 二大要件，其中情節要包含三大元素：背景 (background)、前提 (premise) 與任務 (task)。這類寫作並不困難，重點是讀懂題目，透過分析背景、理解前提，確定寫作任務的方向，針對素養命題的要件與元素，搭配著掌握二十分鐘輕鬆寫作的心法，任何題目皆能得心應手，得高分也就指日可待。

接著，先看以下例子，認識什麼是素養導向情境式命題：

一、看圖寫作

★賣場週年慶

提示：請觀察以下某家賣場週年慶的新聞報導照片，並根據圖片內容想像其中發生的一連串故事，寫一篇英文作文，文長約 120 單詞。文分兩段，第一段描述兩張圖片中所呈現的場景，以及正在發生的狀況或事件；第二段則敘述該事件（或故事）接下來的發展和結果。 (109 學測)

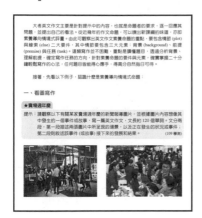

分析

analysis	background	premise	task
plot	某家賣場的週年慶	賣場週年慶的描寫	1. 描述排隊隊伍和人潮擁擠的場景 2. 敘述事件發展和結果
clue	左邊的上方出現 news，下方用中文字標 瘋賣：避開門一搶購	1. 排隊等候開始搶購 2. 現場人山人海	解決問題了？空著遺憾的看到？

寫作藍圖

Lesson 1
從「素養命題」角度分析多種情境、任務式的大考英文作文。

透過寫作藍圖與表格分析說明，循序漸進建構寫作脈絡。

說明
任每閱讀提示中的每一句說明，圖出重點（如賣場週年慶），第一段必須以說明和圖片為基礎，發揮觀察力描述圖片中的場景及正在發生的事件，即介紹故事背景。第二段則是發揮個人的想像力，有邏輯地為圖片中的故事設計出後續發展與合理的結果。

Step 2. 從認識文體、寫作思考串聯到掌握關鍵句型，逐步打造寫作基本功。

Lesson 2 → Lesson 3 → Lesson 4
介紹大考常見三文體　　帶入寫作三角和轉折用語　　提供寫作萬用句

一般來說，看圖寫作常見的手法是起敘和描寫，故二者都歸屬學會。主題寫作常見的說明文，經常也會加入一段的記敘或描寫。因此，一定要清楚明白這三種文體的寫法。以下兩小段介紹三種文體的特色與寫作技巧，提供題目範例，輔以架構圖幫助寫作者了解寫作脈絡。

一、記敘文 (narrative essays)

1. 依據個人過往親歷的敘述型文章，行的思考建構是能夠了解作者所經歷過的一切。記敘文重點在講述一個故事或事件過去，通常是從自己的角度來敘。

2. 敘述故事一定要有人、事、時、地、物、原因、過程與結果，也就是我們常說到的說法：利用 5W1H(who、what、when、where、why、how) 來回憶故事。

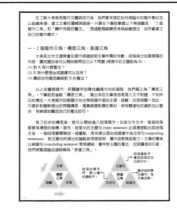

以下提供一段描寫 Lydia 幫祖父母舉辦結婚 30 週年紀念派對的過程，並說明 Lydia 在什麼時間及哪些地點做了些什麼事。

敘述事件記憶中自己三個問題，如：

(1) Who held the celebration? Lydia.
(2) What was special about the celebration? There was a heart-shaped 3-tier cake, each tier with different flavors.
(3) When was the celebration? Last Sunday.

在了解大考常見寫作文體與技巧後，我們要來探討如何將腦中的寫作素材加以組織串連，建立文章的邏輯與脈絡。只要在下筆前掌握以下兩個重點：「2 個寫作三角」和「轉折用語的魔法」，透過動筆鍛鍊思考與組織邏輯，自然會建立自己的寫作模式。

一、2 個寫作三角：構思三角、表達三角

大考英文作文常會著重在提升明確說明文章所需的字數，段落與段落要撰寫的內容。講完題目後只要簡地問自己三個問題（將提不的主題設為 X）：
(1) 對 X 有什麼想法？
(2) X 有什麼理由或觀點可以支持？
(3) 最終如何綜結歸納 X 的看法？

以上從審視提示、抓題鍵字到尋找編寫方向的過程，我們稱之為「構思三角」。下筆前著手「構思三角」，寫出來的文章容易落落不到重點、不知所云的情況。X 有寫作的解題方向也增與思考的段落、結論、反思相關。只要針對相關的出問題構思、電筆鍵詞寫的素材，再有組織地把資訊加以歸納，有條理地闡述自己的看法說明。

有了初步的構思思考，就可以開始進入段落寫作。在英文寫作中，每一個段落都要有清楚的主旨。首先，段落中的主旨句 (topic sentence) 必須清楚開點在該段中主旨。一個段落要闡述一個重點，再支持出由給說理提作為支持句 (supporting sentences)。對主旨句所提出的論點做深度說明，讓內容更具說服力。文章的最後以結論句 (concluding sentence) 緊抵連結，重申對主旨的看法，加深讀者的印象。我們將整個論述過程稱為「表達三角」。

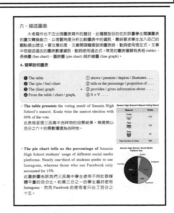

六、描述圖素

大考寫作也不斷出現圖表寫作的題目，此種題型的目的在於評量學生閱讀圖表的圖文轉換能力。以下要翻有數分析出能圖表所呈現出的資訊。要統要求學生加入自己的觀點描述出提法。要注意的是，文章開頭要簡單描述圖表的目的、動詞使用現在式；文中若描述過去的評據時要數據資訊，動詞使用過去式。常見的圖表種類有表格 (table)、長條圖 (bar chart)、圓餅圖 (pie chart) 與折線圖 (line graph)。

A. 簡單說明圖表

❶ The table	① shows / presents / depicts / illustrates ...
❷ The (pie / bar) chart	② tells us the percentage / proportion of ...
❸ The (line) graph	③ provides / gives information about ....
❹ From the table / graph,	④ S + V ...

- The table presents the voting result of Sanmin High School's mascot. Koala wins the mascot election with 60% of the vote.
  此表格呈現三民高中吉祥物的投票結果。無尾熊以百分之六十的得票數當選吉祥物。

- The pie chart tells us the percentage of Sanmin High School students' usage of different social media platforms. Nearly one-third of students prefer to use Instagram, whereas those who use Facebook only accounted for 15%.
  此圓餅圖告訴我們三民高中學生使用不同社群媒體平臺的百分比。約莫三分之一的學生偏好使用 Instagram，然而 Facebook 的使用者只佔了百分之十五。

i

Step 3. 提供大考各類寫作題型技巧剖析與範文，全面提升英文寫作力。

Lesson 5 & 6
深度解密主題、圖表、看圖與信函寫作，從 14 篇範文中學習好用詞彙與句型。

★★★方便學習的三大精心設計★★★

① Extended Writing Map　　② 漸進引導式的寫作練習。　　③ 提供寫作過程與範文的解析。

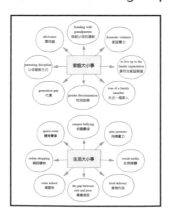

① 提供 7 個 Extended Writing Map，從大考常見主題情境再延伸，共 56 個寫作題材！

② 針對主題、圖表、看圖與信函寫作各提供一個獨立頁面的寫作練習，方便撕下練習與批閱。

③ 解析夾冊內含練習解答、4 篇附題目與寫作大綱的範文，方便攜帶閱讀。

Lesson 1

素養導向情境式評量

一、看圖寫作：賣場週年慶

二、圖表寫作：美國青年關注新聞統計

三、主題寫作：行銷臺灣、排隊現象、
　　　　　　　寂寞經驗

英文素養寫作攻略

　　大考英文作文主要是針對提示中的內容，也就是命題者的要求，逐一回應其問題，並提出自己的看法。從近幾年的作文命題，可以嗅出新課綱的味道，亦即素養導向情境式評量。由此可觀察出英文作文素養命題的重點，要包含情節 (plot) 與線索 (clue) 二大要件，其中情節要包含三大元素：背景 (background)、前提 (premise) 與任務 (task)。這類寫作並不困難，重點是讀懂題目，透過分析背景、理解前提，確定寫作任務的方向，針對素養命題的要件與元素，確實掌握二十分鐘輕鬆寫作的心法，任何題目皆能得心應手，得高分自然指日可待。

　　接著，先看以下例子，認識什麼是素養導向情境式命題：

一、看圖寫作

★賣場週年慶

提示：請觀察以下有關某家賣場週年慶的新聞報導圖片，並根據圖片內容想像其中發生的一個事件或故事，寫一篇英文作文，文長約 120 個單詞。文分兩段，第一段描述兩張圖片中所呈現的場景，以及正在發生的狀況或事件；第二段則敘述該事件 (或故事) 接下來的發展和結果。　　　　　(109 學測)

🔍 分析

analysis	background	premise	task
plot	某家賣場的搶購新聞	賣場週年慶的盛況	1. 描述排隊現場和人潮擁擠的場景 2. 敘述事件發展和結果
clue	左圖的左上角出現news，下方有中文字幕寫著：玻璃門一推開	1. 排隊等候開始營業 2. 現場人山人海	順利解決問題？空留遺憾的省思？

✏️ 寫作藍圖

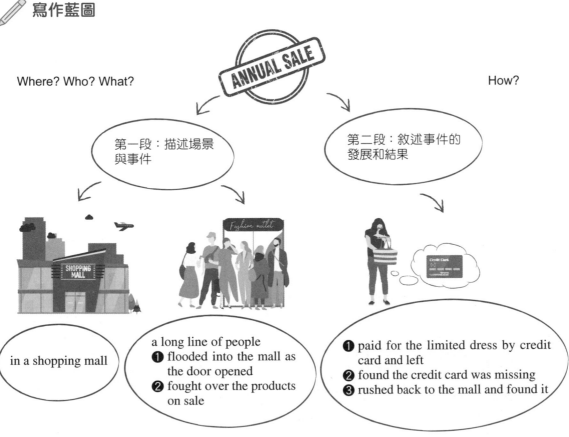

ANNUAL SALE

Where? Who? What?　　　　　　　　　　　　　　　　　How?

第一段：描述場景與事件

第二段：敘述事件的發展和結果

in a shopping mall

a long line of people
❶ flooded into the mall as the door opened
❷ fought over the products on sale

❶ paid for the limited dress by credit card and left
❷ found the credit card was missing
❸ rushed back to the mall and found it

💬 說明

　　仔細閱讀提示中的每一句說明，圈出重點 (如賣場週年慶)，第一段必須以說明和圖片為基礎，發揮觀察力描述圖片中的場景及正發生的事件，即介紹故事背景；第二段則是發揮個人的想像力，有邏輯地為圖片中的故事設計出後續發展與合理的結果。

①主題情境：賣場週年慶
②第一段：描述兩張圖片場景與可能發生的事件

場景 (Where)	in a shopping mall
人物 (Who)	a long line of people
事件 (What)	❶ flooded into the mall as the door opened ❷ fought over the products on sale

③第二段：敘述接下來的發展與結果

發展 (How)	❶ paid for the limited dress by credit card and left ❷ found the credit card was missing ❸ rushed back to the mall and found it

二、圖表寫作

★美國青年關注新聞統計

提示：右表顯示美國 18 至 29 歲的青年對不同類別之新聞的關注度統計。請依據圖表內容寫一篇英文作文，文長至少 120 個單詞。文分二段，第一段描述圖表內容，並指出關注度較高及偏低的類別；第二段則描述在這六個新聞類別中，你自己較為關注及較不關注的新聞主題分別為何，並說明理由。

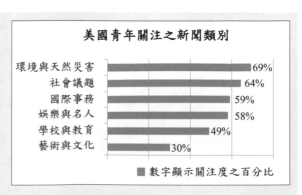

美國青年關注之新聞類別

環境與天然災害 69%
社會議題 64%
國際事務 59%
娛樂與名人 58%
學校與教育 49%
藝術與文化 30%

■ 數字顯示關注度之百分比

(108 指考)

分析

analysis	background	premise	task
plot	美國青年對不同類別新聞的關注度統計	圖表	1. 描述圖表中關注度較高及偏低的類別 2. 描述自己關注與不關注的新聞類別，並說明理由
clue	六種新聞類別	新聞類別與關注度百分比	1. 數據分析與比較 2. 依據題意說明理由

寫作藍圖

What?　　　　　　　　　　　　　　　　　　　　　　What? Why?

Chart analysis

第一段：指出關注度最高與最低的新聞類別

第二段：陳述自己的新聞關注類別狀況並說明理由

| the most concerning | the least concerning | the most concerning | the least concerning |

the environmental and natural disasters

social issues

art and culture

the environmental and natural disasters

the entertainment and celebrity news

說明

　　仔細閱讀提示中的每一句說明，圈出重點，第一段必須以圖表為基礎，點出圖表類型與呈現的資料，並明確指出美國青年關注度較高與偏低的新聞類別。第二段依據題意選出自己關注及不關注的新聞類別，進而闡述自己的看法。

①主題情境：閱讀圖表闡述想法
②第一段：描述圖表內容，指出關注度最高及最低的類別

內容 (What)	The most concerning categories: ❶ the environmental and natural disasters (69%) ❷ social issues (64%) The least concerning category: art and culture (30%)

③第二段：敘述自己關注與不關注的新聞類別並分別說明理由

類別 (What)	The most concerning category: the environmental and natural disasters The least concerning category: the entertainment and celebrity news
理由 (Why)	Reasons for choosing the environmental and natural disasters: ❶ under threats of pollution and natural disasters ❷ promote environmental awareness Reasons for choosing the entertainment and celebrity news: ❶ celebrities' private lives are irrelevant to us ❷ pay much attention to the global issues

三、主題寫作

★行銷臺灣

提示：身為臺灣的一份子，臺灣最讓你感到驕傲的是什麼？請以此為題，寫一篇英文作文，談臺灣最讓你引以為榮的二個面向或事物 (例如：人、事、物、文化、制度等)。第一段描述這二個面向或事物，並說明它們為何讓你引以為榮；第二段則說明你認為可以用什麼方式來介紹或行銷這些臺灣特色，讓世人更了解臺灣。

(108 學測)

分析

analysis	background	premise	task
plot	臺灣有許多的特色	引以為榮的	1. 描述二個面向並說明原因 2. 說明行銷臺灣特色的方式
clue	感到驕傲的	人、事、物、文化、制度等	讓世人更了解臺灣

寫作藍圖

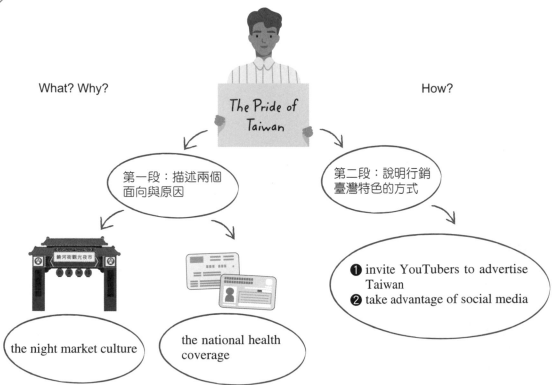

What? Why?

The Pride of Taiwan

How?

第一段：描述兩個面向與原因

第二段：說明行銷臺灣特色的方式

❶ invite YouTubers to advertise Taiwan
❷ take advantage of social media

the night market culture

the national health coverage

💬 說明

　　仔細閱讀提示中的每一句說明，圈出重點，可利用第一句說明成為第一段下筆的主題句，而支持句提供的例子與原因就是你的個人經驗。第二段說明用哪些方式來介紹、行銷這些臺灣特色，讓世人更了解臺灣。

①主題情境：臺灣特色
②第一段：描述二個面向及原因

面向 (What)	Two features: the night market culture and the national health coverage
原因 (Why)	The night market culture: ❶ a wide range of delicious street food ❷ shopping ❸ entertainment The national health coverage: ❶ the leading universal healthcare system ❷ low medical fees

③第二段：說明行銷臺灣特色的方式

方法 (How)	Ways of promoting Taiwan: ❶ invite YouTubers to advertise Taiwan ❷ take advantage of social media

★排隊現象

提示：排隊雖是生活中常有的經驗，但我們也常看到民眾因一時好奇或基於嘗鮮心理而出現大排長龍 (form a long line) 的現象，例如景點初次開放或媒體介紹某家美食餐廳後，人們便蜂擁而至。請以此種一窩蜂式的「排隊現象」為題，寫一篇英文作文。第一段，以個人、親友的經驗或報導所聞為例，試描述這種排隊情形；第二段，說明自己對此現象的心得或感想。

(107 學測)

🔍 **分析**

analysis	background	premise	task
plot	排隊是生活常有經驗	民眾因好奇或基於嘗鮮心理	1. 描述排隊現象 2. 說明心得與感想
clue	景點初次開放或媒體介紹某家美食餐廳	1. 排隊經驗 2. 新聞報導	一窩蜂式的「排隊現象」

✏️ **寫作藍圖**

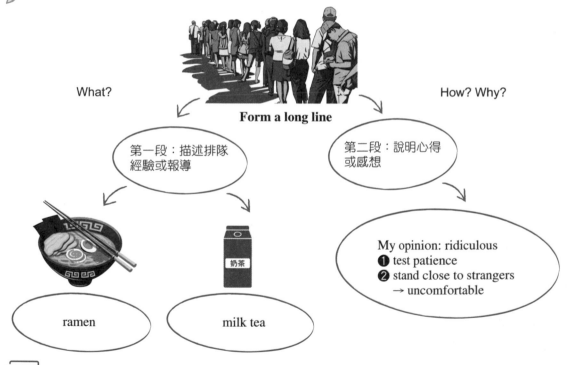

What?

How? Why?

Form a long line

第一段：描述排隊經驗或報導

第二段：說明心得或感想

ramen

milk tea

奶茶

My opinion: ridiculous
❶ test patience
❷ stand close to strangers
→ uncomfortable

💬 **說明**

　　仔細閱讀提示中的每一句說明，圈出重點，其中英文提示 (form a long line) 一定要運用在文章中，可利用第一句說明成為第一段下筆的主題句，並以你的經驗或新聞報導為例加以補充說明。第二段的主題句可先表述自己對排隊的看法，再進一步闡述原因支持你的論點。

📝 英文素養寫作攻略

①主題情境：排隊現象
②第一段：描述排隊經驗或報導

排隊經驗或報導 (What)	Examples: ❶ a long line of ramen worshipers ❷ the craze for milk tea

③第二段：說明心得或感想

心得或感想 (How)	My opinion: ridiculous
原因 (Why)	Reasons: ❶ test patience ❷ stand close to strangers → uncomfortable

★寂寞經驗

提示：每個人從小到大都有覺得寂寞的時刻，也都各自有排解寂寞的經驗和方法。當你感到寂寞時，有什麼人、事或物可以陪伴你，為你排遣寂寞呢？請以此為主題，寫一篇英文作文，文長至少 120 個單詞。文分兩段，第一段說明你會因為什麼原因或在何種情境下感到寂寞，第二段描述某個人、事或物如何伴你度過寂寞時光。

(106 指考)

🔍 分析

analysis	background	premise	task
plot	每個人都有覺得寂寞的時刻	排解寂寞	1. 說明你會寂寞的原因 2. 說明如何度過寂寞時光
clue	排解寂寞的經驗和方法	陪伴你的人、事或物	何種情境：說個故事

✏️ **寫作藍圖**

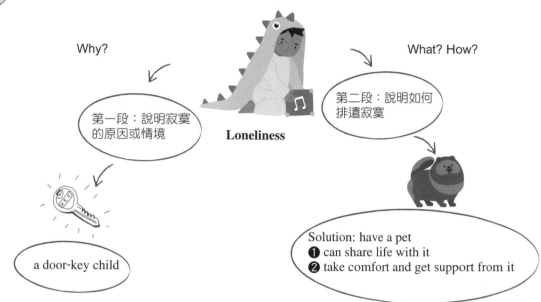

Why?

What? How?

第一段：說明寂寞
的原因或情境

第二段：說明如何
排遣寂寞

Loneliness

a door-key child

Solution: have a pet
❶ can share life with it
❷ take comfort and get support from it

💬 **說明**

　　仔細閱讀提示中的每一句說明，圈出重點，甚至可以利用第一句「每個人從
小到大都有寂寞的時刻」成為第一段下筆的主題句，再娓娓道來自己的寂寞經
驗。第二段則著重描述故事的轉折點──排遣寂寞的關鍵人、事或物及如何度過
寂寞時光。

①主題情境：寂寞
②第一段：寂寞的原因

原因 (Why)	Reason: a door-key child

③第二段：如何排遣寂寞 (經驗)

關鍵人事物 (What)	Have a pet
如何排遣 (How)	Ways of relieving loneliness: ❶ can share life and joy with it ❷ take comfort and get support from it

英文素養寫作攻略

　　從以上題目可以歸納出，大考英文作文偏重於情境式的素養命題，主要評量學生是否能針對需求，整合其閱讀理解、圖表判讀、資訊應用、批判思考能力，靈活運用文字應答 what、why、how 等 Wh- 疑問。而題目所對應的文體常是說故事的記敘文 / 描寫文 (narrative / descriptive essays)、說明原因及設法解決問題的說明文 (expository essays)。

 Your Turn!

■ 人因夢想而偉大，請以此為主題，畫出寫作藍圖。第一段說明你的夢想為何；第二段舉例說明你要如何做才能達成這個夢想。

🖊 **寫作藍圖**

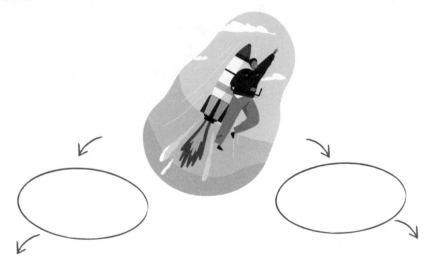

Lesson 2

大考常用三文體

一、記敘文
二、描寫文
三、說明文

　　一般來說，看圖寫作常見的手法是記敘和描寫，故二者都要學會。主題寫作常見的說明文，經常也會加入一段的記敘或描寫。因此，一定要清楚明白這三種文體的區別。以下將分別介紹三種文體的特色與寫作技巧，提供題目範例，輔以架構圖幫助寫作者了解寫作脈絡。

一、記敘文 (narrative essays)

1. 依據個人經驗撰寫的敘述型文章，目的是希望讀者能夠了解作者所經歷過的一切。記敘文重點在講述一個故事的來龍去脈，通常是從自己的角度來看。

2. 敘述故事一定要有人、事、時、地、物、原因、過程與結果，也就是我們常聽到的說法：利用 5W1H(who、what、when、where、why、how) 來回應故事。

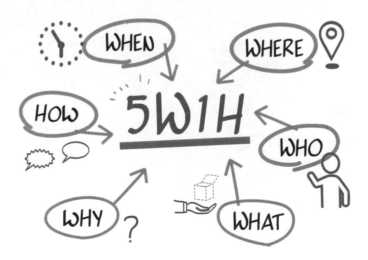

　　以下提供一段描寫 Lydia 幫祖父母舉辦結婚 50 週年紀念派對的過程，並說明 Lydia 在什麼時間及哪個地點做了些什麼事。

　　說故事要記得問自己六個問題，如：
(1) Who held the celebration? <u>Lydia.</u>
(2) What was special about the celebration? <u>There was a heart-shaped 3-tier cake, each tier with different flavors.</u>
(3) When was the celebration? <u>Last Sunday.</u>

(4) Where did the celebration take place? <u>In the yard.</u>

(5) Why did Lydia hold the celebration? <u>For her grandparents' 50th wedding anniversary.</u>

(6) How did Lydia's grandparents feel about the celebration? <u>They felt very happy.</u>

　　當我們很清楚心中的答案，就能輕鬆寫下簡單的記敘文：

　　Last Sunday was the 50th wedding anniversary of Lydia's grandparents; therefore, she held a small but memorable celebration in the yard for them. Lydia made them a heart-shaped 3-tier wedding cake as a gift. Each tier has different flavors. Vanilla was on the top, key lime was in the middle, and chocolate was at the bottom. Her grandparents were very happy because the cake was exactly what they loved. That was an unforgettable day in their lives.

3. 有時記敘文也會精心挑選事件中的細節來鋪陳展現主題，其段落通常按時間順序編寫。

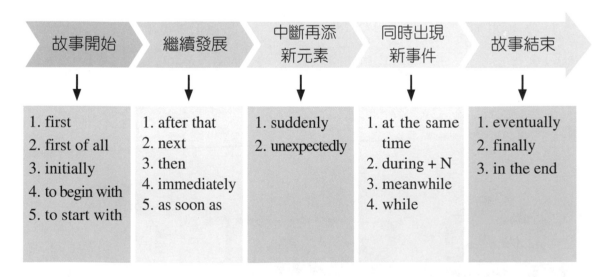

故事開始	繼續發展	中斷再添新元素	同時出現新事件	故事結束
1. first 2. first of all 3. initially 4. to begin with 5. to start with	1. after that 2. next 3. then 4. immediately 5. as soon as	1. suddenly 2. unexpectedly	1. at the same time 2. during + N 3. meanwhile 4. while	1. eventually 2. finally 3. in the end

　　當你熟記這五組表達時間順序的轉折詞時，敘述一個經驗或事件會更加得心應手。

Try it!

從下列選項中，選出最適當的時間轉折詞，填入空格中。

An Unforgettable Trip to Japan

Last December, I took a trip to Japan with my sister. __1__ , we flew to Hokkaido by budget airline. __2__ we arrived in Hokkaido, we were amazed by the snow-covered scenery. It was sunny but freezing cold outside, and __3__ we checked in at the hotel near the airport. After that, we went out for a walk and got some takeout food for lunch. __4__ , a flock of loud crows flew around us, trying to steal food from my hand. My sister was so scared that she used her umbrella to scare them away.

We enjoyed some breathtaking scenery and local cuisine __5__ these days. The last night in Sapporo, we stopped by the mini Christmas market at Odori Park. __6__ we were hunting for souvenirs, a Santa Claus was walking toward us. "Merry Christmas!" he smiled and said. He leaned forward and gave us a big warm hug. We even took a selfie with him. That was such a special experience! I can't wait to visit Hokkaido again soon!

| (A) As soon as | (B) While | (C) Suddenly |
| (D) during | (E) First | (F) then |

1. _____   2. _____   3. _____
4. _____   5. _____   6. _____

4. 一個故事的結尾通常會為生活帶來影響或啟發。因此，記敘文的結論有以下常見寫法：

類型	例句
A. 感想	· With mom's love, my heart was full and happy. 有了母親的愛，我的心充滿了快樂。
B. 期望	· I hope never to lose confidence in myself. 我希望永遠不要對自己失去信心。
C. 啟示	· Never again did Sue judge a book by its cover. Sue 再也不會以貌取人。
D. 勉勵	· Having no fear, our team is sure to win next year. 毫無恐懼，明年我們的隊伍肯定會獲勝。

5. 技巧總匯：
   (1) 主題句須明確點出文章主題，即該人物、事件或物品的重要性，以引起讀者興趣。
   (2) 敘述的內容要清楚表達故事的來龍去脈 (人、事、時、地、物)，可善加利用對話內容 (引述句)、說話者的臉部表情或動作的描述，讓讀者更有臨場感、文章更加生動。
   (3) 依據事件發生的時間順序來描寫故事，並適時使用轉折語。
   (4) 結論可使用感想、期望等寫法總結，再次點明文章主旨。

二、描寫文 (descriptive essays)

1. 描寫文最大的特點在於善用五種身體感官 (視覺、味覺、嗅覺、觸覺和聽覺) 去觀察細節，有條理地去構思布局段落，主要目的是要讓讀者能透過寫作者的文字去想像、感同身受。描寫的內容可以是真實的經驗或是虛構的故事。

2. 描寫文除了可使用感官多角度去描繪勾勒出人物或景物生動的細節特徵外，也可使用比喻、擬人、誇飾等修辭手法來增強讀者的感官體驗。

(1) 視覺的描述：

　　‧It is a town of forest with thousands of tall trees standing along the roadside.
　　　這是一個森林小鎮，有數千棵高大的樹木聳立在路邊。

(2) 嗅覺的描述：

　　‧Gina's hair smelled like gorgeous roses mixed with fresh mints.
　　　Gina 的頭髮聞起來像華麗的玫瑰混合著清新的薄荷糖。

(3) 味覺的描述：

　　‧This overcooked lamb chop tasted like rubber.
　　　這道煮過頭的羊排嘗起來像橡皮。

(4) 觸覺的描述：

　　‧Her face became soft and smooth after she applied the moisturizing cream.
　　　在塗完潤膚霜後，她的臉變得柔軟平滑。

(5) 聽覺的描述：

　　‧The angry lady roars like thunder, and you can hear her from far away.
　　　那位憤怒的女子如雷聲般的怒吼，你在遙遠的地方都可聽見。

(6) 使用修辭法：

　　‧My smartphone is my soulmate. It keeps my photos, music collection, and
　　　secrets. It accompanies me throughout my daily life. I can't live without it.
　　　我的智慧型手機是我的靈魂伴侶。它保有我的照片、歌單和祕密。它陪伴
　　　我度過每一天。沒有它我就活不下去。(隱喻和擬人)

3. 描寫文有時會在文章結尾帶入內心的感受，讓描寫的主題深深烙印在讀者的腦海裡。
   · I am forever respectful toward my father who has fought to keep others alive, and to this day I am proud to say, "Dad, you're my hero."
   我永遠尊敬我的父親為了讓別人活著而奮鬥，直到今天，我很自豪地說：「爸，你是我的英雄。」
   · I would like to visit Rome again, for it is the place that reminds me what happiness is.　我想再次拜訪羅馬，因為它讓我想起幸福的模樣。

4. 技巧總匯：
   (1) 運用身體五感去觀察，試著從不同角度抓住描寫對象的特徵。
   (2) 適時巧用比喻、擬人、誇飾等多種修辭讓筆下的人事物更生動，躍然紙上。
   (3) 結尾可延伸張力加入內心的感受，讓讀者對寫作者產生共鳴，加深對描寫主題的印象。

 Try it!

請找出下列句子中使用感官描述或修辭法的部分，並將它們劃上底線。
1. The final exam week is a nightmare for Sam. He has been bombarded with tests and assignments from six classes.
2. Your words are like a sharp knife cutting my heart into millions of pieces.
3. During holidays, I enjoy taking a walk into the woods, listening to the natural symphony played by the birds, frogs, and insects.

三、說明文 (expository essays)

1. 針對特定主題提供相關訊息，例如描述現象、比較分類、說明過程、理由、看法，或是討論因果關係等，目的是讓讀者在看文章後能明白所要說明的事物。應掌握的寫作重點有三項：
   (1) 開場從說明主題開始，引言的介紹應該簡短，但提供的內容資訊要精準、充分。

(2) 接著主體通常會依據說明對象的不同，採取不同的寫作形式 (如逐步列舉、比較與對比、討論因果等) 來進行觀點陳述，有條理地安排與主題相關的具體細節來佐證自己的說明。

(3) 結論須在文末依據前面的論述提出總結，但此時不宜再提出任何新的觀點，以免模糊論述焦點。

2. 說明文主體常見的寫作形式有以下幾種：

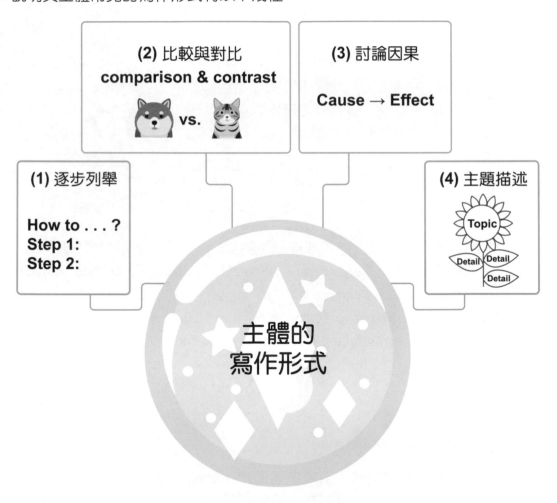

(1) 逐步列舉：此類型寫作主要在向讀者解釋如何逐步列舉、分階段地達成目的這一整個過程。寫作者要依照邏輯順序提供所有訊息，以便讓讀者循著文章脈絡逐步完成任務。

範例：How to Plan a High School Graduation Party (如何規劃高中畢業派對)

How to Plan A High School Graduation Party

Step 1	choose a theme and set a budget
Step 2	make a memorable slide show with music and photos
Step 3	select decorations and a music playlist
Step 4	schedule the entertainment

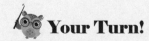 **Your Turn!**

■ 請說明如何準備升學面試。
■ 請說明如何製作讀書計劃。

(2) 比較與對比：這種寫作形式主要針對兩項事物進行比較與對比，找出相似與不同之處，以便讓讀者了解各自的特點或利弊。
範例：Online shopping vs. In-store shopping (線上購物 vs. 店內購物)

Ways of Shopping	Online shopping	In-store shopping
Similarities	1. can pay by cash or credit card 2. have seasonal sales and promotion	
Advantages	1. avoid crowds and save time 2. compare prices easily, and shop anywhere at any time 3. have more product choices and less pressure from the sales staff	1. can see, touch, and try on the product 2. can get the product you bought right away 3. do not worry about shipping
Disadvantages	1. have risks of buying defective products 2. receive products that are below expectations 3. worry about the leakage of personal information	1. spend too much time finding the best deal between stores or waiting in line 2. have limited product options 3. restricted to opening hours

 Your Turn!

■ 說明穿制服與穿便服上學的差異。
■ 闡述跟團旅遊和自助旅行的優缺點。

(3) 討論因果：此種寫作方式有兩種，一種是說明造成此種現象的原因是什麼，另一種則是此種現象會帶來什麼樣的影響或後果。

範例 (因)：The Causes of Forming a Long Line (大排長龍的原因)

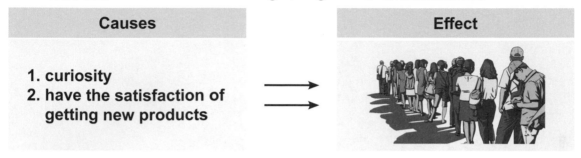

範例 (果)：The Effects of Global Warming (全球暖化的影響)

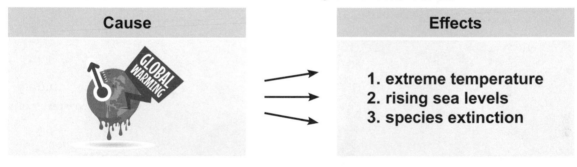

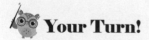 **Your Turn!**

■ 說明假新聞氾濫的原因。
■ 說明網路成癮對現代人的影響。

(4) 主題描述：描述性的說明文主要針對主題給予定義或解釋，並提供具體事件、人物、地點、想法等細節描述。這種寫作形式常見於請同學從生活經驗切入主題以此延伸，藉由提出事實、舉例描述等方式來說明自己的想法。
範例：My Ideal Day Trip from Taiwan (我理想的臺灣一日遊地點)

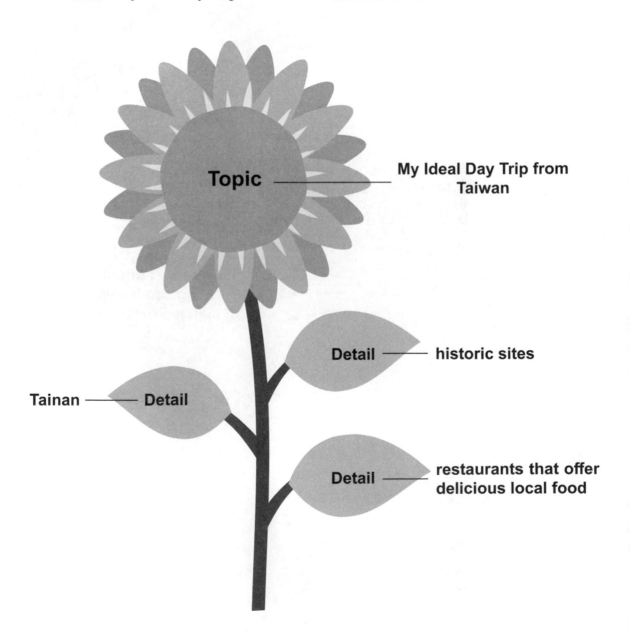

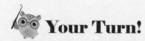 **Your Turn!**

■ 描述家庭中的家事分配狀況並說明你的看法。
■ 描述校園風雲人物的特徵並說明你對成為校園風雲人物的看法。

3. 說明文與議論文的差異：
   說明文與議論文寫作主要都是針對主題說明，但二者在寫作角度以及文章架構還是有些許的差異，請見下表說明：

文體	說明文 (expository essays)	議論文 (argumentative essays)
寫作角度	1. 針對主題探討各種角度 2. 偏向客觀，採取中立 3. 通常以第三人稱表達	1. 針對主題表達贊成或反對的論點 2. 偏向主觀，需選定立場 3. 通常以第一人稱表達
文章架構	1. 主題句：對主題提出明確的解釋或說明 2. 主體：提供步驟、例子或理由等細節去支持你的說明 3. 結論：換句話說再次強調說明主題	1. 主題句：直接表明支持或反對論點 2. 主體：依據所選立場提出論據以支持和證明你的論點 3. 結論：換句話說，再次強調你的論點
例子	How COVID-19 Affected My Life (新冠肺炎如何影響我的生活)	Should Artificial Intelligence Be Regulated? (人工智慧是否應該被規範？)

Note

Lesson 3

寫作思考與串聯

一、2 個寫作三角：構思三角、表達三角

二、轉折用語的魔法

在了解大考常見寫作文體與技巧後，我們要來探討如何將腦中的寫作素材加以組織串連，建立文章的邏輯與脈絡。只要在下筆前掌握以下兩個觀念：「2 個寫作三角」和「轉折用語的魔法」，透過勤寫鍛鍊思考與組織想法，自然會建立自己的寫作模式。

一、2 個寫作三角：構思三角、表達三角

大考英文作文通常會在提示明確說明文章所需的字數、段落與分別要撰寫的內容，讀完題目後可以開始詢問自己以下問題 (將提示的主題設為 X)：
(1) 對 X 有什麼看法？
(2) X 有什麼理由或證據可以支持？
(3) 最終如何概括總結對 X 的看法？

以上從審視提示、抓關鍵字到尋找編寫方向的過程，我們稱之為「構思三角」。下筆前若省略「構思三角」，寫出來的文章很容易落入文不對題、不知所云的情況。大考寫作的解題方向也常與寫作者的主張、經驗、反思相關。因此，只要針對題幹提出的問題構思、蒐集篩選對應的素材，將有關連性的資訊加以整合，有條理地闡述自己的看法即可。

有了初步的構思後，就可以開始進入段落寫作。在英文作文中，每個段落都要有清楚的架構。首先，段落中的主題句 (topic sentence) 必須清楚點出該段落主旨，一個段落簡單陳述一個重點，再來提出理由或證據作為支持句 (supporting sentences)，對主題句所提出的論點做深度說明，讓內容更具說服力。文章的最後以結論句 (concluding sentence) 聚焦總結，重申對主題的看法，加深讀者的印象，我們將整個論述過程稱為「表達三角」。

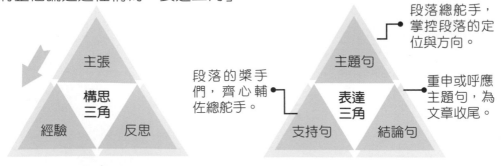

主題句	如同段落的總舵手,掌控段落的定位與方向。主題句由「主題」與「中心論點」所構成,通常以簡單的句子明確道出該段落的重點。
支持句	如同段落的槳手們,齊心輔佐總舵手——主題句,藉由提供具體的例子或細節來補充說明延續論述。
結論句	末段的結論句通常以不同於主題句的表達方式去重申或呼應前面所提出的觀點,為文章收尾。

運用「表達三角」所提出的寫作重點,以「如何維護校園安全」為題,擬出主題句、支持句與結論句,請參考以下範例:

主題句:

When it comes to promoting school safety, I believe that building a strict visitor management system seems to be the first priority.

(主題句的主題是 promoting school safety,中心論點是 building a strict visitor management system,明確指出維護校園安全的首要之務是建立嚴謹的訪客管理系統。)

支持句:

(1) The strict visitor management system can verify the visitor's identity and keep track of all the people at school.

(2) The strict visitor management system increases the protection of people at school and reduces the risks of external threats.

(支持句提出具體的細節來補充說明建立嚴謹訪客系統的優點。)

結論句:

Only with a strict visitor system can we provide students and teachers a secure environment.

(結論句再次重申主題句的論點,總結只有嚴謹訪客系統才能真正提供師生一個安全的環境。)

Try it!

運用「表達三角」所提出的寫作重點，以「如何戰勝憂鬱」為題，請試著擬出主題句、支持句與結論句。

主題句：
1.＿＿＿＿＿＿＿＿＿＿＿＿＿＿＿＿＿＿＿＿＿＿＿＿＿＿＿＿＿＿

＿＿＿＿＿＿＿＿＿＿＿＿＿＿＿＿＿＿＿＿＿＿＿＿＿＿＿＿＿＿＿

支持句：
2.＿＿＿＿＿＿＿＿＿＿＿＿＿＿＿＿＿＿＿＿＿＿＿＿＿＿＿＿＿＿

＿＿＿＿＿＿＿＿＿＿＿＿＿＿＿＿＿＿＿＿＿＿＿＿＿＿＿＿＿＿＿

3.＿＿＿＿＿＿＿＿＿＿＿＿＿＿＿＿＿＿＿＿＿＿＿＿＿＿＿＿＿＿

＿＿＿＿＿＿＿＿＿＿＿＿＿＿＿＿＿＿＿＿＿＿＿＿＿＿＿＿＿＿＿

結論句：
4.＿＿＿＿＿＿＿＿＿＿＿＿＿＿＿＿＿＿＿＿＿＿＿＿＿＿＿＿＿＿

＿＿＿＿＿＿＿＿＿＿＿＿＿＿＿＿＿＿＿＿＿＿＿＿＿＿＿＿＿＿＿

二、轉折用語的魔法

對寫作者而言，轉折用語是一篇作文的魔法師，適當地善用它們可以畫龍點睛。轉折用語不但能有邏輯地引領讀者從上一個想法進入到下一個想法，亦擔負起串聯者的角色，將兩個句子或段落做層次分明、脈絡清楚的銜接，使文章更為通順流暢。無論是記敘文、描寫文或各種類型的說明文，只要能掌握好轉折用語，寫作魔法就瞬間出現。以下介紹常見種類的轉折用語，並實際應用它們在段落中，一起來感受轉折用語的魔力吧！

1. 順序

此類轉折用語通常用來表達時間或空間上的先後順序，例如描述事件發展的過程、步驟等，或是依據文章所要強調的重點來排序論述。關於順序的常見轉折用語如下：

A. 起始、列舉順序	B. 接續	C. 結尾
· at first	· afterward	· as a final point
· first of all	· after	· at last
· for a start	· after that	· eventually
· first, second, third . . .	· before long	· finally
· in the (first, second, third . . .) place	· later	· in the end
· initially	· later on	· last but not least
· to start with	· next	· lastly
· to begin with	· subsequently	· to conclude
	· then	· to sum up

Yesterday was the first time that I cooked at home. While cooking fish, I accidentally dripped a little drop of water into the pan and my left hand got burned. I could not help screaming because it was painful! On hearing my voice, my mom came to the kitchen and turned off the stove immediately. I was made to cool the burn under the cold running water for ten minutes. She took out some ice cubes from the refrigerator and wrapped them with a handkerchief. She asked me to apply it to the injured skin with care. I've learned a lesson that I can never be too careful while cooking.

加入順序類轉折用語，讓文章產生魔力，讀一下感受其差異：

Yesterday was the first time that I cooked at home. While cooking fish, I accidentally dripped a little drop of water into the pan and my left hand got burned. I could not help screaming because it was painful! On hearing my voice, my mom came to the kitchen and turned off the stove immediately. In the beginning, I was made to cool the burn under the cold running water for ten minutes. Then, she took out some ice cubes from the refrigerator and wrapped them with a handkerchief. After that, she asked me to apply it to the injured skin with care. In the end, I've learned a lesson that I can never be too careful while cooking.

Try it!

請試著從下方挑選適當的順序類轉折用語，並填入空格中：

Friendship plays an essential role in our life. How to choose friends wisely is a lesson that everyone should learn. For me, good friends have three characteristics. __1__, good friends are good listeners. When I'm in a bad mood, they can listen to my worries and help me cope with sadness without judging me. __2__, good friends are sincere and honest. When I'm doing wrong, they won't criticize me behind my back. Instead, they will talk to me directly and we will find solutions together. __3__, good friends will motivate me to challenge myself and progress. They encourage me to step out of my comfort zone and push me to achieve goals. __4__, making friends with people who have these three characteristics can be of benefit to us.

(A) Third	(B) Second	(C) To sum up	(D) First of all

1. _____ 2. _____ 3. _____ 4. _____

2. 因果

此類轉折用語通常用來表達原因、結果或是某種條件或前提下產生的後果。關於因果的常見轉折用語如下：

A. 原因	B. 結果	C. 條件 → 後果
• as、for、since	• accordingly	• as long as / so long as
• because (of the fact that)	• as a consequence	• even if
• being that	• as a result	• granted (that)
• due to (the fact that)	• consequently	• if、if not、if so
• for the reason that	• hence	• in that case
• inasmuch as	• so	• in the event that
• in that	• therefore	• on (the) condition that
• in view of (the fact that)	• thus	• otherwise
• owing to (the fact that)		• under . . . circumstances
• seeing that		• unless

Nowadays, childhood obesity has been a serious problem. Obese children are not only unhealthy but also easily being teased or bullied in school. This may lead to low self-esteem and psychological distress without being treated well. Most working parents have no time to cook proper meals, they often take their children to eat out at fast food restaurants without realizing the damaging effects of greasy food. What's worse, children spend more time sitting in front of screens than exercising outdoors. Excess intake of calories and lack of exercise are the causes of children's obesity. Parents make an effort to build healthy eating and exercise habits for children, curbing childhood obesity will not be difficult.

加入因果類轉折用語或將部分字詞以此類轉折用語轉換，讓文章產生魔力，讀一下感受其差異：

Nowadays, childhood obesity has been a serious problem. Obese children are not only unhealthy but also easily being teased or bullied in school. This may lead to low self-esteem and psychological distress if not treated well. Since most working parents have no time to cook proper meals, they often take their children to eat out at fast food restaurants without realizing the damaging effects of greasy food. What's worse, children spend more time sitting in front of screens than exercising outdoors. Thus, excess intake of calories and lack of exercise are the causes of children's obesity. As long as parents make an effort to build healthy eating and exercise habits for children, curbing childhood obesity will not be difficult.

Try it!

請試著從下方挑選適當的因果類轉折詞，並填入空格中：

    If someone hurts you badly, you naturally feel angry and even think of revenge. It is a common problem that many people are struggling with these negative emotions. Nevertheless, forgiveness may be the best option __1__ it can set you free from negative emotions and bad thoughts. Before you forgive someone, you have to face the facts and work through your emotions. When realizing that what has occurred cannot be changed, you accept that the painful events are history and that there is no beneficial effect of constant suffering on you. You might not want any kind of relationship with the people who hurt you anymore, __2__ you don't have to punish them, either. __3__ you make a decision to stop the anger, you are also freed from the burden of self-condemnation. __4__, you will feel relieved because you have replaced negative emotions with peace. Forgiveness cannot change the past, but it can change your future.

(A) Consequently   (B) So long as   (C) because   (D) but

1. _____   2. _____   3. _____   4. _____

3. 比較與對比

    下方左欄的轉折用語通常用於比較兩者的共同點，而右欄所列的轉折用語則是用以突顯句子前後對比的差異。關於比較與對比常見轉折用語如下：

A. 比較	B. 對比	
• by the same token	• but	• nevertheless
• equally	• however	• nonetheless
• in comparison with	• in contrast	• though
• in the same way	• instead	• whereas
• likewise	• on the contrary	• while
• similarly	• on the other hand	• yet

Text messaging has affected teenagers' written language. In fact, cellphones' tiny keypads make them get used to using shorthand for efficiency. For example, 881 means goodbye, since the numbers sound like "bye-bye" when pronounced in Chinese. 520 replaces "I love you," 530 means "I miss you." Using shorthand for fast replies seems convenient. Some educators worry that teenagers' writing may go from bad to worse if they continue to ignore grammar rules in favor of speed. 4 better or worse, shorthand is here 2 stay.

加入比較與對比類轉折用語，讓文章產生魔力，讀一下感受其差異：

Text messaging has affected teenagers' written language. In fact, cellphones' tiny keypads make them get used to using shorthand for efficiency. For example, 881 means goodbye, since the numbers sound like "bye-bye" when pronounced in Chinese. Similarly, 520 replaces "I love you," while 530 means "I miss you." Using shorthand for fast replies seems convenient. However, some educators worry that teenagers' writing may go from bad to worse if they continue to ignore grammar rules in favor of speed. 4 better or worse, shorthand is here 2 stay.

Try it!

請試著從下方挑選適當的比較與對比類轉折用語，並填入空格中：

More and more people are used to having a cup of coffee as a refreshing beverage every morning. Scientists from different fields, __1__, have diverse opinions on the effects of drinking coffee. Some specialists suggested that frequent coffee intake can reduce the risk of diabetes. __2__, psychologists have found evidence that caffeine in coffee can help people stay more focused and work more efficiently. __3__, other health professionals warned that the caffeine in coffee would stimulate the kidney, causing people to pass water more. Meanwhile, people who have coffee lose infection-fighting vitamins and minerals, __4__ becoming vulnerable and easily getting a cold. Although the findings seem to be contradictory, keeping a moderate intake of coffee may be the proper way to stay healthy.

(A) Likewise	(B) In contrast	(C) however	(D) thus

1. _____ 2. _____ 3. _____ 4. _____

4. 舉例、補充與強調

A-1. 舉例	**B-1. 補充**	**C-1. 強調**
· for example · for instance · including · such as · take . . . for example	· additionally · along with · also · furthermore · in addition · moreover	· apparently · clearly · in particular · notably · obviously · undoubtedly
A-2. 換句話說	**B-2. 關於**	**C-2. 事實上**
· in other words · namely · that is (to say) · to put it another way	· concerning · in terms of · with regard to · with respect to	· actually · as a matter of fact · indeed · in fact

Although Taiwan is located near Japan, the two nations are actually very different. The Taiwanese tend to be more carefree than the Japanese in social manners. Japanese people will usually not say "NO" even if their real intention is to refuse. Taiwanese people might do the opposite. They will directly turn down the invitations. Some Taiwanese on the subway talk loudly on the phone without paying attention to others around them. But in Japan, people on the subway are careful about the noises and refrain from talking on the phone. It is interesting to see how the two countries so close on a map can have cultural habits that are so far apart. Living in the global village, we should respect and embrace these cultural differences.

加入舉例、補充與強調類的轉折用語或將部分字詞以這些類別的轉折用語轉換，讓文章產生魔力，讀一下感受其差異：

Although Taiwan is located near Japan, the two nations are actually very different. In terms of social manners, the Taiwanese tend to be more carefree than the Japanese. For example, Japanese people will usually not say "NO" even if their real intention is to refuse. In fact, Taiwanese people might do the opposite. That is to say, they will directly turn down the invitations. In addition, some Taiwanese on the subway talk loudly on the phone without paying attention to others around them. But in Japan, people on the subway are careful about the noises and refrain from talking on the phone. It is interesting to see how the two countries so close on a map can have cultural habits that are so far apart. Undoubtedly, living in the global village, we should respect and embrace these cultural differences.

Try it!

請試著從下方挑選適當的轉折用語，並填入空格中：

Is your glass half-empty or half-full?   1 , do you look on the bright or dark side of the matter in a tough situation? We all have bad days in our life. But if we try to look at difficulties from a different angle, the outcome might be different.   2 , imagine as follows: You are in the dumps and arguing with your parents. You may react quite differently depending on how you deal with the uncomfortable feeling. First, you can leave the house and slam the door. Then you notice you are in an even worse mood because the anger has ruined your entire day. In this case, your glass is "half-empty." Your day is unlikely to improve since you only experience the feeling of loss.

The second way to react is with your glass "half-full." You can try to realize that the fight with your parents is common. Even parents have their bad days, too! Then why not make each other feel better and make up? You will   3   feel the day is bright and full of possibilities once you let go of the anger. This simple example   4   can serve as a mirror through which you evaluate your life. Would you rather drown in sorrow when you can cherish half a glass of joy and peace, or you embrace the bad feelings and get over the pain soon?

(A) indeed	(B) For instance	(C) also	(D) In other words

1. _____ 　 2. _____ 　 3. _____ 　 4. _____

Lesson 4

寫作常用關鍵句型

通常大考寫作會有哪些命題呢？先看以下的分析：

考試年度	主題	第一段	第二段	分析
111 學測	理想公園樣貌	圖 A 和圖 B 的公園各有何特色	說明你心目中理想公園的樣貌與特色	1. 說明文 2. 說明文
110 學測	遊客賞花公德心	看圖描述遊客到訪某場所的新聞圖片內容	以遊客或場所主人的立場表達看法	1. 描寫文 2. 說明文
110 指考	大學專業課程英語授課	說明你對這個現象的看法	若未來大學必修課以英語授課，如何因應或規劃	1. 說明文 2. 說明文
109 學測	賣場週年慶	看圖描述某家賣場週年慶的場景及事件	敘述該事件或故事接下來的結果	1. 描寫文 2. 記敘文
109 指考	維護校園安全	說明校園安全重要性及校園可能發生的安全問題	說明校內成員應採取哪些作為以維持校園安全	1. 說明文 2. 說明文
108 學測	行銷臺灣	描述兩個臺灣讓你引以為榮的面向或事物	行銷臺灣特色的方法	1. 說明文 2. 說明文
108 指考	美國青年對新聞關注度	描述圖表內關注度較高與偏低的類別	描述自己較關注與較不關注的類別並說明理由	1. 說明文 2. 說明文
107 學測	排隊現象	以個人、親友經驗或新聞報導為例描述排隊情形	對此現象的心得或感想	1. 記敘文 2. 說明文
107 指考	社區活動三選一	說明你的選擇與原因	你認為應該要有的活動內容與設計理由	1. 說明文 2. 說明文
106 學測	看連環圖說故事	描述前三張出遊遇到塞車與人潮情境	自由發揮描述完整的結局	1. 描寫文 2. 記敘文
106 指考	寂寞經驗	說明造成你寂寞的原因或情境	描述你如何排解寂寞	1. 說明文 2. 說明文
105 學測	家事分工	說明你對家事分工的看法或理由	舉例說明你做家事的經驗及感想	1. 說明文 2. 說明文
105 指考	高學歷找工作	說明此現象的成因	如何因應？舉例說明你對大學生涯的學習規劃	1. 說明文 2. 說明文

　　由上表中得知，大考常出現的寫作為記敘文、描寫文、說明文等三種文體，其中以說明文出現的頻率最高。針對以上的命題及文體分析，下方歸納出一些可運用於大考寫作的關鍵句型。每個公式下方提供兩個與歷屆大考作文主題相關的例句，幫助同學從情境脈絡了解句型的使用：

一、表達「提出看法」

❶ As far as + N + is concerned,　　　　① I think / suppose that . . . .

❷ When it comes to + V-ing / N,　　+　② I believe that . . . .

❸ Speaking of + V-ing / N,　　　　　　③ I am deeply convinced that . . . .

· **When it comes to** promoting school safety, **I believe that** building a strict visitor management system seems to be the first priority.
說到促進校園安全，我相信建立一個嚴謹的訪客管理系統為首要之務。

· **Speaking of** household chores, **I think that** all the family members should share the responsibilities.
談到家事，我認為所有家庭成員都應該一起共同承擔。

二、表達「陳述理由」

A. 單一理由

❶ Because / Since / Now that / Given that + S + V, ...
❷ Because of / Due to / Owing to / Thanks to + N / V-ing, ...

· **Since** school security is closely related to students' safety, we should take any potential threats seriously.
因為校園安全與學生的安全息息相關，我們應該認真對待任何潛在威脅。

· **Due to** the popularity of the Internet, the government can produce online promotional films to attract tourists from all over the world.
由於網路普及性，政府可以製作一些線上宣傳片藉以吸引世界各地的觀光客。

B. 兩個或兩個以上的理由

❶ One reason is that . . . . The other is that . . . .
❷ One is that . . . . Another is that . . . .

· There are two reasons why I often feel lonely. **One reason is that** I live alone without my family's support. **The other is that** I am too shy to make friends.
我時常感到孤獨的原因有兩個。一個是我一人獨自生活少了家人的支持。另一個則是我生性害羞無法交友。

· There might be multiple causes for high-educated people to apply for waste collector jobs. **One is that** our education tends to focus on testing rather than developing skills. **Another is that** high education no longer guarantees getting a high-paying job.
高學歷的人應徵清潔隊員工作的原因可能有很多。一個是我們的教育傾向於重視考試多於培養技能。另一個則是高學歷不保證能取得高薪工作。

三、表達「感想、心得或反思」

❶ It's a(n) . . . experience to V . . . .
❷ With such a(n) . . . experience, S + V . . . .
❸ This . . . experience has changed . . . .
❹ After . . . , I feel . . . .

· **It's an** unpleasant shopping **experience to spend** so much time lining up for limited lucky bags.
為了限量福袋排隊而花費這麼多時間是一次很不愉快的購物經驗。

· **This** summer internship **experience has changed** my perspective on future careers.
這次暑期實習經驗改變了我對未來職業的看法。

四、表達「事件或人物帶來的影響」

❶ A + have a(n) . . . influence / impact / effect + on + B . . . .
❷ B + has influenced / affected + A . . . .

· Keeping a pet **had an enormous influence on** my childhood life. Not only could I share joy and sorrow with it but also got emotional support from it.
養寵物為我童年生活帶來巨大的影響。我不僅可以與牠同甘共苦，也從牠身上得到情感上的支持。

43

- Aging population **has** profoundly **affected** social and economic development. We cannot overemphasize the importance of home care services for seniors.
人口老化已深度影響社會與經濟發展。為老人提供居家照護的重要性再怎麼強調也不為過。

五、舉例說明

❶ For example / instance, ...
❷ Take . . . for example / instance, ...
❸ To give a clear example / instance, ...
❹ To illustrate an example / instance of . . . .

- An increasing number of foreign YouTubers produce videos promoting Taiwan's features. **For example**, the Israeli Internet celebrities made a clip featuring Taiwan's tourist attractions, natural landscapes, and convenience.
越來越多國外的 YouTuber 拍片行銷臺灣的特色。例如：以色列網路名人拍了一支短片以臺灣旅遊景點、自然景觀和便利為特色。

- This chart shows that the environment and natural disasters are the most concerning issues among young Americans. **To give a clear example**, in recent years many deadly tornadoes have occurred in the US, causing numbers of deaths and injuries.
這份圖表顯示環境與天然災害是美國青年最關注的議題。舉一個明顯的例子，近年來許多致命的龍捲風發生在美國，造成眾多人傷亡。

六、描述圖表

　　大考寫作也不乏出現圖表寫作的題目，此種題型目的在於評量學生閱讀圖表的圖文轉換能力，以客觀角度分析比較圖表中的資訊，最終要求學生加入自己的觀點提出想法。要注意的是，文章開頭簡要說明圖表時，動詞使用現在式。文章中若描述過去的圖表數據資訊，動詞使用過去式。常見的圖表種類有表格 (table)、長條圖 (bar chart)、圓餅圖 (pie chart) 與折線圖 (line graph)。

A. 簡單說明圖表

❶ The table	① shows / presents / depicts / illustrates . . . .
❷ The (pie / bar) chart	② tells us the percentage / proportion of . . . .
❸ The (line) graph +	③ provides / gives information about . . . .
❹ From the table / chart / graph,	④ S + V . . . .

· **The table presents** the voting result of Sanmin High School's mascot. Koala wins the mascot election with 60% of the vote.
此表格呈現三民高中吉祥物的投票結果。無尾熊以百分之六十的票數獲選為吉祥物。

Sanmin High School's Mascot Voting Result

Mascot	Votes
Koala	216
Tiger	120
Bear	24
Total Number of Votes	360

· **The pie chart tells us the percentage of** Sanmin High School students' usage of different social media platforms. Nearly one-third of students prefer to use Instagram, whereas those who use Facebook only accounted for 15%.
此圓餅圖告訴我們三民高中學生使用不同社群媒體平臺的百分比。約莫三分之一的學生偏好使用 Instagram，然而 Facebook 的使用者只佔了百分之十五。

Sanmin High School: Social Media Platform Use

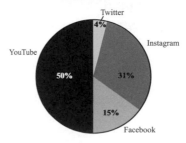

Twitter 4%
Instagram 31%
YouTube 50%
Facebook 15%

B. 減少、降低

❶ The number / percentage of N + decreased / fell / declined . . . .
❷ There was a dramatic (戲劇化的) / massive (大量的) / steady (持續的) + decrease / fall / decline . . . .

· From this line graph, we can see **there was a massive decrease** in sales of cold drinks in winter in 2020.

  從這張折線圖，我們可看出 2020 年冬季冷飲的銷售大量的減少。

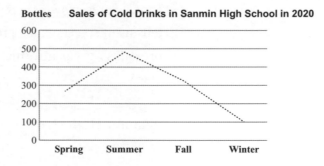

C. 增加、成長

❶ The number / percentage of N + increased / grew / rose . . . .
❷ There was a noticeable (顯著的) / sharp (急遽的) / slight (少量的) + increase / growth / rise . . . .

· **The number of** hot drink sales **had** significantly **increased** from fall to winter in 2020.

  熱飲的銷售數量從 2020 年秋季到冬季大幅地上升。

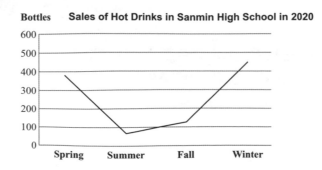

D. 比較

❶ Compared with / In comparison to A, B . . . .
❷ A + be V / V + 比較級 + than + B . . . .
❸ A + be V / V + twice / three / etc. times + as + Adj. + as + B . . . .

· **Compared with** Japanese teenagers, Taiwanese teenagers spend less time on sports and outside reading.
與日本青少年相較，臺灣青少年花費較少的時間在運動和課外閱讀。

· In terms of time spending on sports, Japanese teenagers **spend three times as much as** Taiwanese teenagers.
就花在運動的時數而言，日本青少年所花的時間長度是臺灣青少年的三倍。

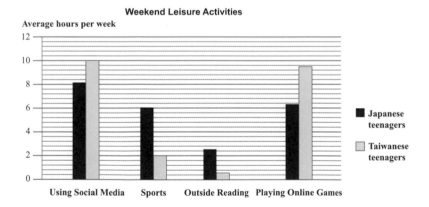

E. 結論

❶ We can conclude that . . . .
❷ Overall / In conclusion / To sum up, ...

· **We can conclude that** students buy cold drinks when the weather gets hotter.
我們可以推斷出學生在天氣變熱時會買冷飲。

· **To sum up,** the weather affects the sales of different drinks.
結論為天氣會影響不同飲料的銷量。

Try it!

克漏式翻譯，每格限填一字。

1. 就減重而言，我深信適度的運動比間歇性斷食來的有效。

   ＿＿＿＿＿＿ ＿＿＿＿＿＿ ＿＿＿＿＿＿ weight loss is concerned, I am deeply convinced that moderate exercises are more effective than intermittent fasting.

2. 因為車輛廢氣排放與空氣汙染密切相關，通勤族被鼓勵多搭乘大眾運輸。

   Commuters are encouraged to take public transportation ＿＿＿＿＿＿ vehicle exhaust is highly relevant to air pollution.

3. 許多年輕人偏好使用社群媒體多於面對面溝通的原因有很多。一個是社群媒體讓他們方便即時聯繫朋友。另一個則是社群媒體可以讓他們傳遞在真人面前不方便表達的意見。

   Many teenagers prefer social media to face-to-face communication for several reasons. ＿＿＿＿＿＿ is that social media makes it convenient for them to reach their friends instantly. ＿＿＿＿＿＿ is that social media enables them to express whatever they feel too awkward to express in front of a real person.

4. 出國念書不僅是在海外上課。學生必須要克服語言與文化障礙。有了這難忘的經驗，他們將學習如何在異鄉自己做決定與解決問題。

   Studying abroad is more than taking classes overseas. Students have to overcome both language and cultural barriers. ＿＿＿＿＿＿ such a memorable experience, they will learn how to make decisions and solve problems by themselves in a foreign country.

5. 此長條圖提供我們資訊關於日本與臺灣青少年每週末花在特定娛樂活動的時數。

   The ＿＿＿＿＿＿ chart ＿＿＿＿＿＿ information about the hours that Japanese and Taiwanese teenagers spend doing certain leisure activities per weekend.

6. 結論是日本和臺灣青少年的週末已逐漸被社群媒體與線上遊戲佔據。

   ＿＿＿＿＿＿ ＿＿＿＿＿＿, both Japanese and Taiwanese teenagers' weekends have become dominated by social media and online games.

Lesson 5

二十分鐘輕鬆寫作文：
大考剖析篇

一、個人抒發：寂寞經驗

二、家庭議題：家事分工

三、社會觀察：賣場週年慶、排隊現象、
　　　　　　　高學歷找工作

四、創意發想：行銷臺灣、社區活動三
　　　　　　　選一

英文素養寫作攻略

　　想要具體提升英文寫作能力，除了要具備 2 個寫作三角所強調的構思及表達組織能力外，還要能活用寫作技巧，例如：善用轉折用語與關鍵句型串聯論點 (說明文)、事件的連結與轉折 (記敘文與描寫文)，讓文句更通順。平日也要藉由不斷地閱讀、觀察社會時事議題，培養對文字的敏銳度，提升用字遣詞能力，不斷地練習寫作。唯有實際下筆才能真正訓練思考、表達與解決問題的能力。若想在大考寫作拿高分，觀摩歷屆大考佳作，了解命題趨勢，掌握各種主題與不同文體的寫作要領更是不可或缺之一環。

　　面對分秒必爭的大考，要如何安排寫作時間呢？在考場上通常建議預留二十分鐘在英文作文，具體的寫作時間分配與操作步驟如下：

三階段	重點說明
規劃 (5 分鐘)	1. 閱讀提示： 　❶ 分析題幹文字、圖片或圖表，解讀題目情境 　❷ 找出關鍵字，確認文章主題 　❸ 理解題目要求，確認寫作範圍，如字數限制、分段必須個別回答的問題等 2. 找出對策： 　在符合題幹要求下，確認答題方向，尋找寫作素材 (如個人經驗、圖表中的統計數字等細節)，分點條列出可能用到的單字或簡短句子。 3. 組織架構： 　利用寫作藍圖組織文章脈絡與層次。
下筆 (13 分鐘)	開始寫作： 依據寫作藍圖的架構，一個段落一個重點。文章必須要有： 　❶ 主題句：清楚表明論點 　❷ 支持句：提出明確的例子、理由、事實、數據或細節支持論點 　❸ 結論句：重申論點呼應主題句，為段落作總結 　❹ 適當使用轉折用語讓句子間更有連貫性，使讀者更容易抓到重點
修改 (2 分鐘)	檢查優化： 寫完後建議預留時間檢查內容是否切題、拼字、大小寫、標點符號、時態等文法是否使用正確。建議使用精準、有把握的單字或片語替換不確定的字詞，減少拼字錯誤、單字誤用而被扣分的情況。

　　我們先從熟悉歷屆大考試題下手，分析命題趨勢，按部就班掌握解題要點。解題四步驟如下：

Step 1. 讀懂題目：閱讀提示，找關鍵字，理解問題
Step 2. 擬定大綱：構思靈感，彙整想法，組織寫作素材，開始擴寫
Step 3. 參考範文：從範文中學習如何鋪陳論述、組織文章結構與拿捏遣詞用句
Step 4. 寫作攻略：練習使用範文中的必學好句或好字，並將其實際運用於自己的
　　　　　文章中

　　依循上述步驟練習後，可請老師批改作文或與同學交換批閱，討論彼此寫作優缺點。每篇大考試題後方也提供 Extended Writing Map，可作為該主題延伸寫作練習的素材。

一、個人抒發

★寂寞經驗

提示：每個人從小到大都有覺得寂寞的時刻，也都各自有排解寂寞的經驗和方法。當你感到寂寞時，有什麼人、事或物可以陪伴你，為你排遣寂寞呢？請以此為主題，寫一篇英文作文，文長至少 120 個單詞。文分兩段，第一段說明你會因為什麼原因或在何種情境下感到寂寞，第二段描述某個人、事或物如何伴你度過寂寞時光。

(106 指考)

Step 1. 讀懂題目

閱讀提示說明，理解其問題：
1. 從文字閱讀中找到關鍵字：寂寞
2. 從文本中找到可用的資訊：什麼人、事或物可以為你排遣寂寞
3. 第一段 (說明)：說明什麼原因或何種情境下感到寂寞
4. 第二段 (說明)：說明如何排遣寂寞
5. 結論：成功度過寂寞時光

 英文素養寫作攻略

Step 2. 擬定大綱

A. 寫作藍圖

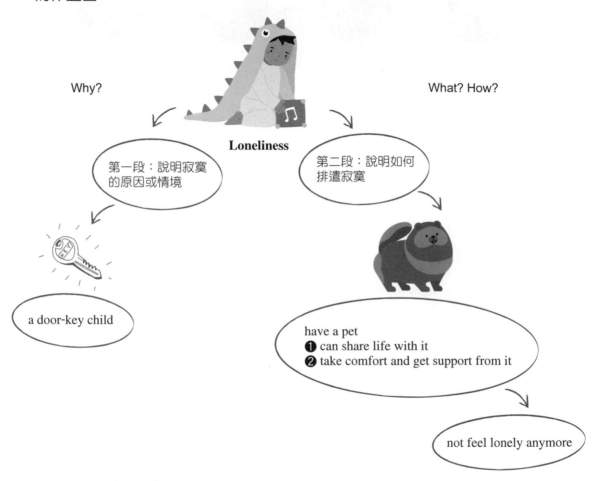

Why?　　　　　　　　　　　　　　　　What? How?

Loneliness

第一段：說明寂寞的原因或情境

第二段：說明如何排遣寂寞

a door-key child

have a pet
❶ can share life with it
❷ take comfort and get support from it

not feel lonely anymore

B. 從寫作藍圖持續擴寫

主題句	無疑地，每個人都有寂寞的感覺。
第一段	說明寂寞的原因或情境： 父母工作時常晚歸，成了鑰匙兒童，感到寂寞
第二段	說明如何排解寂寞：收到狗當生日禮物 ❶ 照顧牠與牠分享生活 ❷ 從牠身上得到安慰與支持
結論句	有寵物的陪伴，再也不會感到寂寞了。

Step 3. 參考範文

Without a doubt, everyone has a feeling of loneliness. Having lived with grandparents in the country before six, I had got so much love and attention from them. Not until I went back to the city to receive education did I know the feeling of loneliness. Ever since then, I had often been **immersed** in silence with a sense of loss. It was at school that I could have fun with my classmates. But after school, I became a door-key child, spending long afternoons alone at home. Before my parents returned home from work, what I could do was just turn on the TV to watch cartoons to relieve loneliness.

Luckily, my **lonely** days didn't last long. My parents gave me the cure for my eighth birthday. "Here's your gift," they said and handed me a cardboard box. I opened it with excitement and care. To my great surprise, inside was an adorable **shaggy** dog. "Its name is Otis. We just adopted it from the shelter," Dad said. Since then, the little dog has become a part of my life. Now the first thing I do after school is look for Otis. Feeding it and sharing my school life with it have been a **routine** of mine. I also take comfort and get support from it. Otis is to me as a child is to a mother. In the **company** of such a lovable dog, I won't feel lonely anymore.

　　無疑地，每個人都有寂寞的感覺。六歲之前和祖父母一起在鄉下生活，我從他們身上得到滿滿的愛與照顧。直到我回到城市接受教育才知道寂寞的感覺。從那時起，我經常沉浸在寂靜及帶有失落感的氛圍裡。在學校，我可以和同學一起玩得很開心。但放學後，我成了鑰匙兒童，獨自在家度過數個漫長的下午。我的父母下班回家前，我能做的就是打開電視看卡通來緩解寂寞。

　　幸運的是，我孤獨的日子並沒有持續多久。我的父母在我八歲生日時給我良方。「這是你的禮物。」他們說，並遞給我一個紙箱。我激動並小心翼翼地打開它。讓我非常驚訝的是，裡面是一隻可愛且毛髮蓬亂的狗。「牠的名字是 Otis。我們剛從收容所收養牠。」爸爸說。從那時起，小狗就成了我生活的一部分。現在放學後我做的第一件事就是尋找 Otis。餵牠並與牠分享我的校園生活一直是我的例行工作。從牠身上我找到安慰與得到支持。Otis 之於我就如同小孩之於母親一樣。有這麼討人喜歡的狗陪伴，我不會再感到寂寞了。

Step 4. 寫作攻略

A. 必學好句

1. Not until I went back to the city to receive education did I know the feeling of loneliness. 直到我回到城市接受教育才知道寂寞的感覺。

> ✏️ 善用 **Not until . . . + 助動詞 + S + V . . . .** 表示「直到…才…」。

直到下午四點 Carol 才完成她的作業。
→ _____

2. Otis is to me as a child is to a mother. Otis 之於我就如同小孩之於母親一樣。

> ✏️ 善用 **A is to B as C is to D**，表達類比譬喻。

火鍋之於冬天就如同冰淇淋之於夏天一樣。
→ _____

B. 必學好字

1. **immerse** *v.* 沉浸
   After breaking up with her boyfriend, Rachel **immersed** herself in her work.
   與男友分手後，Rachel 沉浸於自己的工作中。

2. **lonely** *adj.* 寂寞的
   The old lady lives alone and often feels **lonely**.
   這位老太太獨自生活，經常感到孤獨。

3. **shaggy** *adj.* 毛髮蓬亂的
   The dog with **shaggy** hair is barking at a stranger.
   這隻毛髮蓬亂的狗正在對一位陌生人吠叫。

4. **routine** *n.* 日常生活，例行公事
   Walking the dog for two hours has become a part of David's daily **routine**.
   遛狗兩小時已經成為 David 日常作息的一部分。

5. **company** *n.* 陪伴

I had a wonderful weekend in the **company** of old friends.

我在老朋友的陪伴下度過了一個愉快的週末。

C. Extended Writing Map

二、家庭議題

★家事分工

提示：你認為家裡生活環境的維持應該是誰的責任？請寫一篇短文說明你的看法。文分兩段，第一段說明你對家事該如何分工的看法及理由，第二段舉例說明你家中家事分工的情形，並描述你自己做家事的經驗及感想。

(105 學測)

Step 1. 讀懂題目

閱讀提示說明，理解其問題：
1. 從文字閱讀中找到關鍵字：家事分工
2. 從文本中找到可用的資訊：維持家裡生活環境應該是誰的責任？
3. 第一段 (說明)：說明對家事如何分工的看法及理由
4. 第二段 (說明)：說明自己做家事經驗及感想
5. 結論：做家事的啟示

Step 2. 擬定大綱

A. 寫作藍圖

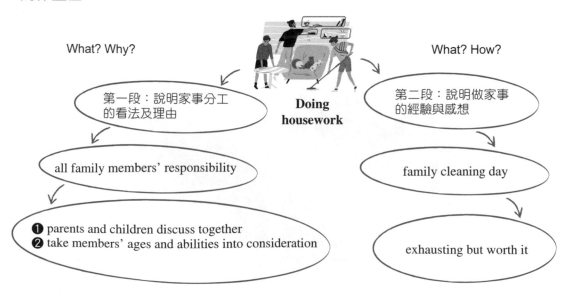

What? Why?　　　　　　　　　　　　　　　　　　What? How?

第一段：說明家事分工的看法及理由　　　Doing housework　　　第二段：說明做家事的經驗與感想

all family members' responsibility　　　　　　　　family cleaning day

❶ parents and children discuss together
❷ take members' ages and abilities into consideration　　　　exhausting but worth it

B. 從寫作藍圖持續擴寫

主題句	既然家是所有家庭成員共同的居住地，每位成員必須為維持一個乾淨的居住環境負責。
第一段	說明家事分工的看法與理由：全家要一起分擔家務 ❶ 鼓勵每個人積極參與：最好是親子討論什麼需要完成，一起計劃 ❷ 依照年紀與能力分配更有效率：人人參與有成就感，營造家庭和諧氛圍
第二段	說明做家事的經驗與感想：每週日是家庭清潔日 ❶ 做家事讓人疲憊不堪 ❷ 享受全家人一起做家事的感覺
結論句	唯有我們共同努力去維持一個乾淨的家，才能讓我感受我們是如此緊密相連。

Step 3. 參考範文

    Since home is a place where all family members live together, every member must be responsible for maintaining a clean living environment. Instead of only relying on one person to clean up the mess, every member should take on **responsibility** for the household **chores**. To encourage the active participation of individuals, it is advisable that parents and children can discuss what needs to be done and make a plan. When dividing household chores, we should take members' ages and abilities into consideration so as to promote efficiency. For instance, young kids or people with poor cooking skills can do the dishes or take out the trash rather than make dinner. If all members are involved and in the right position, housework will be completed soon. Furthermore, sharing household chores gives them a sense of **accomplishment**, which can create a harmonious **atmosphere** at home.

    As for the condition in my family, every Sunday is our family cleaning day. Before cleaning, we will list cleaning tasks for the public area such as vacuuming the living room carpet, cleaning the bathroom, and hanging up the laundry. Then, each of us takes turns choosing tasks that we are good at. After finishing the public area, we will **tidy** our own rooms and make our own beds. Even though doing housework is exhausting, I still enjoy the time doing housework with my family. Only when we work together to maintain a clean home can I feel how close-knit we are.

> 　　既然家是所有家庭成員共同的居住地，每位成員必須為維持一個乾淨的居住環境負責。每一位成員應該要承擔起家事，而非只仰賴一個人去打掃髒亂。為了鼓勵每個人積極參與，最好是雙親和小孩可以討論什麼需要完成，一起計劃。當分配家事時，我們應該將成員的年齡與能力列入考量以提高效率。例如，年紀較小的孩子和廚藝不佳的人可以洗碗或倒垃圾而不是做晚餐。假如每個人都投入且都在正確位置上，家事很快就會被完成。再者，分擔家事給成員們帶來成就感，也能在家中創造一個和諧的氛圍。
>
> 　　我家的狀況是，每週日是我們的家庭清潔日。打掃前，我們會列出公共區域的清潔工作，例如，用吸塵器清掃客廳地毯、打掃廁所和曬衣服。然後，每一個人輪流挑選我們擅長的工作。掃完公共區域後，我們會收拾自己的房間和整理各自的床鋪。即使做家事讓人疲憊不堪，我依舊享受和我家人一起做家事的感覺。唯有我們共同努力去維持一個乾淨的家，才能讓我感受我們是如此的緊密相連。

Step 4. 寫作攻略

A. 必學好句

1. Instead of only relying on one person to clean up the mess, every member should take on responsibility for the household chores.
   每一位成員應該要承擔起家事，而非只仰賴一個人去打掃髒亂。

   ✎ 善用 **Instead of V-ing . . . , S + V . . . .** 表示「不是…，而是…」。

   Peter 總是在週末去健行，而不是待在家。

   → _____

2. Before cleaning, we will list cleaning tasks for the public area such as vacuuming the living room carpet, cleaning the bathroom, and hanging up the laundry.
   打掃前，我們會列出公共區域的清潔工作，例如，用吸塵器清掃客廳地毯、打掃廁所和曬衣服。

   ✎ 善用 **S + V . . . such as A, B, and C.** 列舉 A、B、C 事物補充前面的說明。

Peggy 許下願望來激勵自己表現更好，例如，更努力用功、多運動和存更多錢。

→ _____

B. 必學好字

1. **responsibility** *n.* 責任

   We all have a **responsibility** to preserve aboriginal culture.

   我們都有責任去保護原住民文化。

2. **chore** *n.* 瑣事

   Harrison never helps with the household **chores**.

   Harrison 從未幫忙做家事。

3. **accomplishment** *n.* 成就

   One of Pat's great **accomplishments** is helping the company solve its financial crisis.

   Pat 的偉大成就之一是幫助公司解決財務危機。

4. **atmosphere** *n.* 氣氛

   On New Year's Eve, there is a carnival **atmosphere** on the street.

   新年前夕，街上有狂歡的氛圍。

5. **tidy** *v.* 整理，收拾

   It's time to **tidy** your bedroom!

   該是時候去整理你的臥房了！

C. Extended Writing Map

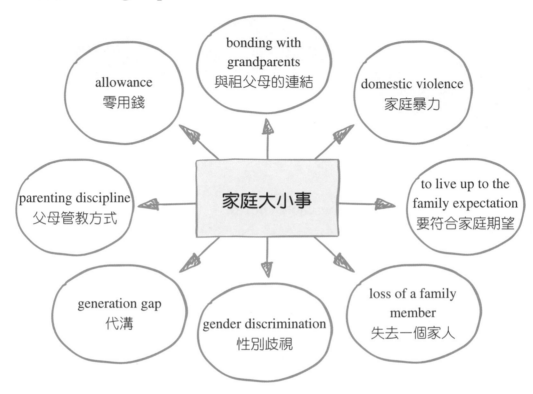

allowance
零用錢

bonding with
grandparents
與祖父母的連結

domestic violence
家庭暴力

parenting discipline
父母管教方式

家庭大小事

to live up to the
family expectation
要符合家庭期望

generation gap
代溝

gender discrimination
性別歧視

loss of a family
member
失去一個家人

三、社會觀察

★賣場週年慶

提示：請觀察以下有關某家賣場週年慶的新聞報導圖片，並根據圖片內容想像其中發生的一個事件或故事，寫一篇英文作文，文長約 120 個單詞。文分兩段，第一段描述兩張圖片中所呈現的場景，以及正在發生的狀況或事件；第二段則敘述該事件 (或故事) 接下來的發展和結果。　　　　　　　(109 學測)

Step 1. 讀懂題目

閱讀提示說明，理解其問題：
1. 從文字閱讀中找到關鍵字：某家賣場週年慶的新聞報導圖片
2. 從文本中找到可用的資訊：想像其中發生的一個事件或故事
3. 第一段 (描寫)：描述兩張圖片中所呈現的場景及正在發生的狀況或事件
4. 第二段 (記敘)：敘述該事件接下來的發展和結果
5. 結論：事件的省思

Step 2. 擬定大綱

A. 寫作藍圖

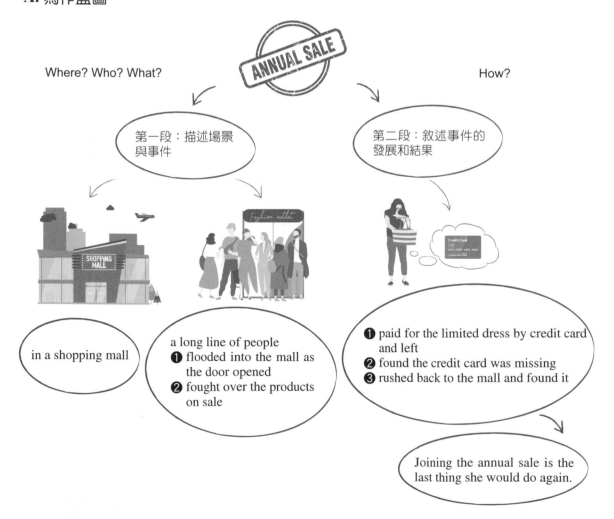

B. 從寫作藍圖持續擴寫

主題句	購物狂每年最期待什麼？週年慶！
第一段	描述圖片中場景與發生的事件： 地點：購物中心 人物：排隊的人潮 事件：❶ 湧入購物中心 　　　❷ 搶特價商品
第二段	敘述事件的發展與結果： ❶ 費盡全力買到限量洋裝離開 ❷ 到家才發現信用卡不見 ❸ 衝回去找到信用卡，雙腿又累又疼
結論句	這個購物經驗給 Kate 學到一個教訓，在週年慶時花長時間排隊是她再也不會做的事了！

Step 3. 參考範文

　　What do shopping lovers look forward to every year? The **annual** sale! There's no denying that anniversary sale promotions always attract thousands of shoppers to make as many purchases as they can. Some of them even line up for several hours before the doors open, and Kate was no exception. Last Saturday, Kate had the chance to join such a big event. **Captivated** by the flyer, she set her heart on a brand-name dress limited in number. To ensure that she could get the item, Kate hurried to the mall in the early morning. When she arrived, out of the blue, there had been a long line of people outside the door. The instant the door opened, a crowd of people flooded into the mall, elbowing their way to get to the targets, just like soldiers in the battlefield fighting the enemy. Kate gasped in **astonishment** at the sight of the shopping rush. All of a sudden, people in the mall were **packed** like sardines. The mall was in total chaos, with shoppers fighting over the products and staff working to keep shoppers in order.

　　But the story didn't end here. To get the limited item, Kate had to try her best to reach the clothes shop. After she finished the shopping trip, Kate gave a sigh of relief. "This was the worst shopping experience I'd ever had," she murmured. However, when getting home, she found her credit card was missing. Controlling her rising **panic**, Kate rushed back to the mall and looked for it. Luckily, the clothing shop staff had found the card and kept it until Kate took it back. Her legs were tired and sore after so much walking. Kate learned from this shopping experience that joining the annual sale is the last thing she would do again!

購物愛好者每年最期待什麼？週年慶！無可否認，週年慶的促銷活動總是能吸引上千名購物者越買越多。其中有些人甚至在開門前排隊等候數小時，而 Kate 也不例外。上週六，Kate 有機會參與這一大盛事。被廣告傳單給吸引，她決心得到一件限量的名牌洋裝。為了確保她能買到，她一大早就匆忙趕去購物中心。當她抵達時，出乎意料地，門外早已大排長龍。門一打開時，一群人湧入購物中心，推擠搶拿他們的目標物，如同在戰場上的軍人衝鋒殺敵般。一看到購物人潮，Kate 吃驚地倒抽一口氣。突然間，購物中心裡的人群擠得跟沙丁魚罐頭似的。購物中心陷入一片混亂，購物者爭搶商品，店員努力維持秩序。

但故事還未結束。為了買到限量商品，Kate 必須盡全力才能抵達服飾店。當她完成了購物之旅，Kate 深深嘆了一口氣。「這是我有史以來最糟糕的購物經驗。」她低語。然而，當她到家時，發現她的信用卡不見了。克制住心中的慌張，Kate 衝回購物中心尋找信用卡。幸運地，服飾店店員早已發現卡片並保留到 Kate 領回。她的雙腿在走那麼多的路後又累又疼。Kate 從這次購物經驗學到一個教訓，參與週年慶是她最不願做的事了！

Step 4. 寫作攻略

A. 必學好句

1. When she arrived, out of the blue, there had been a long line of people outside the door.　當她抵達時，出乎意料地，門外早已大排長龍。

> ✐善用 When + S + V-ed . . . , S + had + p.p. . . . . 描述過去發生的兩個事件。特別要注意的是先發生的用過去完成式，後發生的則用過去簡單式。

當警方到達銀行時，兩名搶匪已經逃跑了。

→ _____

2. Kate learned from this shopping experience that joining the annual sale is the last thing she would do again!

Kate 從這次購物經驗學到一個教訓，參與週年慶是她最不願做的事了！

✎善用 **. . . is the last thing sb would do.** 強調「…是某人最不願做的事」。

放棄鋼琴是 Sam 最不願做的事。

→ _____

B. 必學好字

1. **annual** *adj.* 每年的，一年一度的
   Halloween party is one of my school's **annual** events.
   萬聖夜派對是我學校的年度大活動之一。

2. **captivate** *v.* 使著迷；吸引
   Billy was **captivated** by the stuffed animals in the window.
   Billy 被櫥窗中的絨毛動物玩具給吸引。

3. **astonishment** *n.* 驚訝
   To my **astonishment**, Zoe was laid off because of the factory closure.
   令我驚訝的是，Zoe 因為工廠關閉而被資遣。

4. **pack** *v.* 擠進，塞滿
   Many people **packed** into the supermarket to grab the bargains.
   許多人擠進超市搶奪特價品。

5. **panic** *n.* 恐慌
   Nina got into a **panic** when she found her son was seriously ill.
   當發現她的兒子病得很嚴重，Nina 陷入恐慌。

C. Extended Writing Map

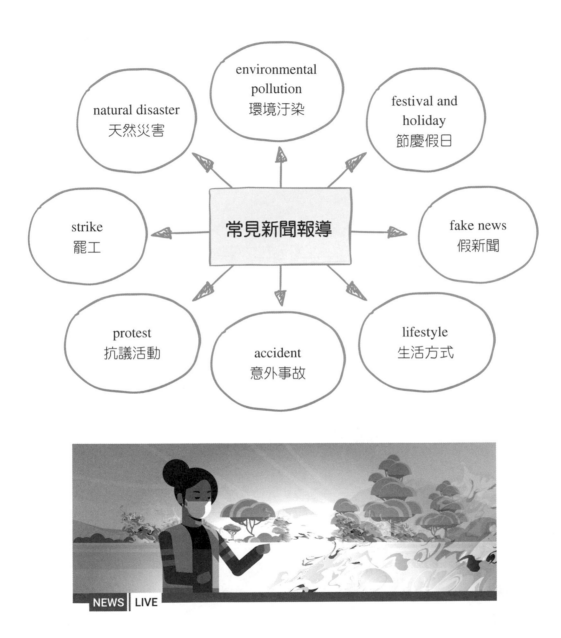

英文素養寫作攻略

提示：排隊雖是生活中常有的經驗，但我們也常看到民眾因一時好奇或基於嘗鮮心理而出現大排長龍 (form a long line) 的現象，例如景點初次開放或媒體介紹某家美食餐廳後，人們便蜂擁而至。請以此種一窩蜂式的「排隊現象」為題，寫一篇英文作文。第一段，以個人、親友的經驗或報導所聞為例，試描述這種排隊情形；第二段，說明自己對此現象的心得或感想。

(107 學測)

Step 1. 讀懂題目

閱讀提示說明，理解其問題：
1. 從文字閱讀中找到關鍵字：排隊現象
2. 從文本中找到可用的資訊：景點初次開放或媒體介紹的美食餐廳
3. 第一段 (記敘)：描述排隊經驗或報導
4. 第二段 (說明)：說明心得或感想
5. 結論：排隊現象的省思

Step 2. 擬定大綱

A. 寫作藍圖

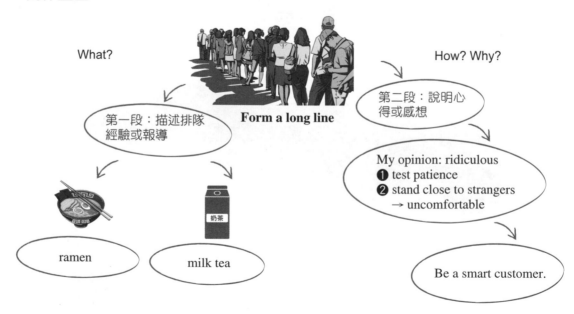

66

B. 從寫作藍圖持續擴寫

主題句	排隊是生活中常見的現象。
第一段	描述排隊經驗或報導： ❶ 拉麵狂熱者排隊 ❷ 奶茶搶購熱潮
第二段	說明心得或感想：這現象可笑且難以忍受 ❶ 考驗耐心 ❷ 與陌生人過於接近不舒服
結論句	不應盲目地跟風，要成為聰明的消費者。

Step 3. 參考範文

Lining up is a common **phenomenon** in life. Because people like to try new things out of **curiosity**, they often spend a lot of time waiting in line for it. According to the news report, a famous ramen restaurant opened its first Taiwan branch in Taipei. It was unlikely for people at that time not to notice a surprising phenomenon: an extremely long line of ramen worshipers was formed in front of the restaurant, which made a new record of its longest continuous queue. Similar craze was also seen when a new beverage was released. Customers formed a long line before the market. As soon as it was opened, crowds of people swarmed to the market and grabbed as many packs of milk tea as possible.

In my opinion, such phenomena are **ridiculous** and unbearable. Standing in line is torture for me. Sweltering in line for hours does test my patience. What's worse, queuing makes the distance between people shorter. Standing close to strangers in a limited space is uncomfortable. Therefore, there's a need for us to stop being manipulated by the media or **influenced** by others. We should resist temptation and consider what we really need. Don't blindly follow the crowd and lose your **identity**! Instead, why not save time in the line and be a smart customer?

> 排隊是生活中常見的現象。由於人們出於好奇心喜歡嘗試新事物，他們時常為此花很長時間去排隊。根據新聞報導，一間知名拉麵餐廳在臺北開了臺灣第一間分店。人們在當時不太可能不去注意的一個令人驚訝的現象：在

餐廳前面形成了一條超長拉麵狂熱者人龍，創造了該餐廳最長的連續排隊記錄。一項新飲品開賣時，也被看見有類似的熱潮。顧客在賣場前排隊。賣場營業的那一刻，人群湧入賣場並盡可能地抓越多組奶茶。

　　在我看來，這種現象是荒謬且難以忍受的。排隊對我來說是折磨。悶熱排隊數小時確實考驗了我的耐心。更糟的是，排隊讓人與人之間距離更短。在有限的空間與陌生人站得很近是不舒服的。因此，我們必須停止被媒體操縱或受他人影響。我們應該抗拒誘惑並仔細思考我們真正需要的是什麼。不要盲目地跟從人群而失去自我！為什麼不節省排隊的時間，做一位明智的消費者呢？

Step 4. 寫作攻略

A. 必學好句

1. It was unlikely for people at that time not to notice a surprising phenomenon.
人們在當時不太可能不去注意的一個令人驚訝的現象。

✐善用 **. . . unlikely . . . not . . . .** 表示「負負得正」的強調效果。

Joanne 不太可能畢業後不去找工作。

→ _____

2. Instead, why not save time in the queue and be a smart customer?
為什麼不節省排隊的時間，做一位明智的消費者呢？

✐善用 **why not + . . . and . . . ?** 反問來強化自己的主張。

為什麼不離開沙發，外出散步呢？

→ _____

B. 必學好字

1. **phenomenon** *n.* 現象
Using social media to express one's opinion is a **phenomenon** of the 21st century.
利用社群媒體表達想法是 21 世紀的現象。

2. **curiosity** *n.* 好奇

Ryan opened his wife's package out of **curiosity**.

Ryan 出於好奇打開了他妻子的包裹。

3. **ridiculous** *adj.* 荒謬的，可笑的

Jasmine looked **ridiculous** in this oversize dress.

Jasmine 穿著這件過大的洋裝看起來很可笑。

4. **influence** *v.* 影響

Colors are said to **influence** the way people feel, think, and even act.

據說顏色會影響人們的感受、思考甚至行為。

5. **identity** *n.* 認同；身分

Wearing a school uniform gives Nancy a sense of **identity**.

穿著校服給 Nancy 帶來認同感。

C. Extended Writing Map

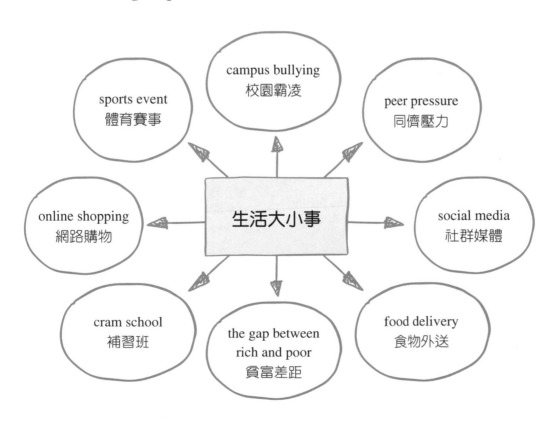

英文素養寫作攻略

★高學歷找工作

提示：最近有一則新聞報導，標題為「碩士清潔隊員 (waste collectors with a master's degree) 滿街跑」，提及某縣市招考清潔隊員，出現 50 位碩士畢業生報考，引起各界關注。請就這個主題，寫一篇英文作文，文長至少 120 個單詞。文分兩段，第一段依據你的觀察說明這個現象的成因，第二段則就你如何因應上述現象，具體 (舉例) 說明你對大學生涯的學習規劃。

(105 指考)

Step 1. 讀懂題目

閱讀提示說明，理解其問題：

1. 從文字閱讀中找到關鍵字：碩士清潔隊員滿街跑
2. 從文本中找到可用的資訊：新聞報導 50 位碩士報考清潔隊員
3. 第一段 (說明)：說明此現象成因
4. 第二段 (說明)：具體舉例說明你對大學生涯的學習規劃
5. 結論：成功因應此現象

Step 2. 擬定大綱

A. 寫作藍圖

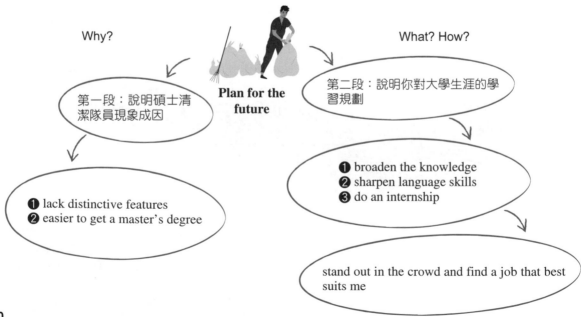

B. 從寫作藍圖持續擴寫

主題句	顯然許多高學歷的人仍然很難找到適合自己興趣和能力的工作。
第一段	說明此現象成因： ❶ 缺乏獨特性，難以突出 ❷ 取得碩士學歷與過去相比較為容易
第二段	說明你對大學生涯的規劃： ❶ 擴展知識：除本領域的主修外，額外上不同領域的課程 ❷ 訓練語言能力：參與活動，培養良好社交能力 ❸ 畢業前實習：獲取寶貴工作經驗
結論句	擁有這些能力或經驗，我相信我將在人群中格外出眾，找到最適合我的工作。

Step 3. 參考範文

The story about 50 people with a master's degree competing for few **vacancies** for waste collectors made headlines. It has already caught the attention of the public. Apparently, many high-educated young people still find it difficult to find jobs that suit their interests and abilities. In my opinion, one factor contributed to this phenomenon is that these people may lack distinctive traits to **distinguish** themselves from others. On top of that, it's easier to get a master's degree compared to the past. Therefore, despite their degree, they have no choice but to apply for this job.

To avoid this situation happening, I will have to prepare myself for future opportunities by making the most of my college life. First and foremost, I will have a thirst for knowledge in the field I major in. At the same time, I will take courses in multiple fields to enrich my learning since broadening the knowledge is indispensable for getting a good job. Next, to have a global **mindset**, I will **sharpen** my language skills and interact with people from different backgrounds. For example, I will be active in a variety of school activities and socialize with international students. I believe this will equip me with excellent interpersonal skills. As the saying goes, "Knowledge is a treasure, but practice is the key to it." As a result, I will seize the opportunity to do an **internship** before graduation to gain valuable work experience. With all these abilities and experience, I'm deeply convinced that I will stand out in the crowd and find a job that best suits me.

關於 50 位碩士畢業生競爭清潔隊員工作空缺的故事成為新聞。它也已經吸引大眾的注意。顯然許多高學歷的年輕人仍然很難找到適合自己興趣和能力的工作。依我所見，其中一個導致這個現象的要素是這群人可能缺乏獨特性難以和他人區分。此外，取得碩士學歷與過去相較較為容易。因此，儘管高學歷，他們別無選擇只能應徵這份工作。

為了避免這個情況發生，我將會充分利用我的大學生活為將來的機會做好準備。首要的是，我將對我主修的領域求知若渴。同時，我將會修不同領域的課程來充實我的學習，因為擴展知識對於取得一個好工作是必不可少的。緊接著，要有全球思維，我會磨練我的語言技能與不同背景的人交流。例如，我會積極參與學校活動與國際學生交際。我相信這會使我擁有良好的社交能力。俗話說：「知識是寶藏，但實踐是其金鑰。」因此，畢業前我會把握機會去實習以獲取寶貴的工作經驗。擁有這些能力或經驗，我相信我將在人群中格外出眾，找到最適合我的工作。

Step 4. 寫作攻略

A. 必學好句

1. Therefore, despite their degree, they have no choice but to apply for this job.
   因此，儘管高學歷，他們別無選擇只能應徵這份工作。

   🖊善用 **S + have no choice but + to V . . . .** 表示「別無選擇只能…」。

   因為大雨，我們別無選擇只能取消戶外活動。
   → _____

2. As the saying goes, "Knowledge is a treasure, but practice is the key to it."
   俗話說：「知識是寶藏，但實踐是其金鑰。」

   🖊善用 **As the saying / proverb goes, ". . . ."** 引用俗話或諺語於寫作，豐富文章內容。

   俗話說：「三思而後行。」
   → _____

B. 必學好字

1. **vacancy** *n.* 空缺

   After careful consideration, Leo decided to look for part-time job **vacancies** online.

   經過仔細考慮後，Leo 決定上網尋找兼職工作空缺。

2. **distinguish** *v.* 使有所區別

   It's Olivia's amazing talent for arts that **distinguishes** her from other competitors.

   Olivia 對藝術驚人的天分與其他競爭者大不相同。

3. **mindset** *n.* 思維；觀念

   Tony was promoted to vice president due to his innovative **mindset**.

   由於他的創新思維，Tony 被升為副總經理。

4. **sharpen** *v.* 加強；增進

   Nelson takes an online course to **sharpen** his speaking skills.

   Nelson 上一堂線上課程來加強他的口說技巧。

5. **internship** *n.* 實習

   Last month, we had an **internship** at a software company.

   上個月，我們在一家軟體公司實習。

C. Extended Writing Map

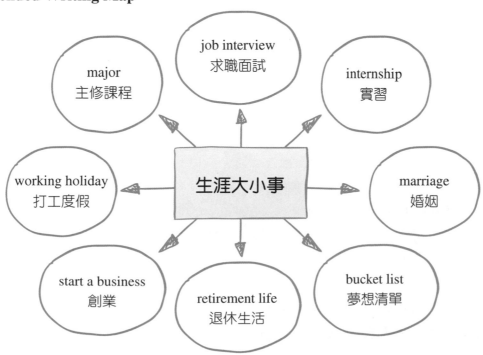

四、創意發想

★行銷臺灣

提示：身為臺灣的一份子，臺灣最讓你感到驕傲的是什麼？請以此為題，寫一篇英文作文，談臺灣最讓你引以為榮的二個面向或事物 (例如：人、事、物、文化、制度等)。第一段描述這二個面向或事物，並說明它們為何讓你引以為榮；第二段則說明你認為可以用什麼方式來介紹或行銷這些臺灣特色，讓世人更了解臺灣。　　　　　　　　　　　　　　　　　(108 學測)

Step 1. 讀懂題目

閱讀提示說明，理解其問題：

1. 從文字閱讀中找到關鍵字：臺灣最讓你感到驕傲的是什麼？
2. 從文本中找到可用的資訊：引以為榮的二個面向或事物
3. 第一段 (說明)：描述二個面向並說明原因
4. 第二段 (說明)：說明行銷臺灣特色的方式
5. 結論：讓世人更了解臺灣

Step 2. 擬定大綱

A. 寫作藍圖

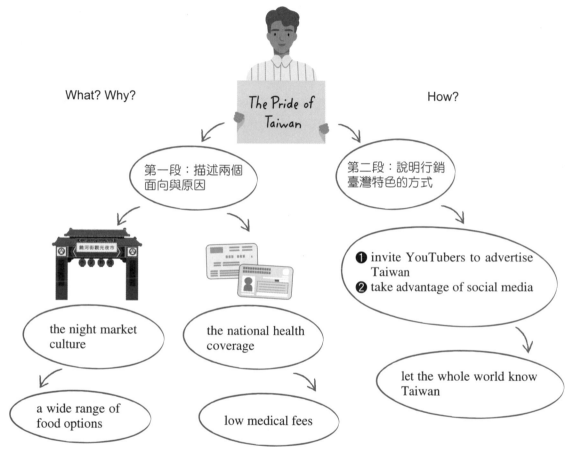

B. 從寫作藍圖持續擴寫

主題句	身為臺灣人，我深深地為我的國家感到驕傲。
第一段	描述二大面向及原因： ❶ 夜市文化：多種美食、娛樂、購物選擇 ❷ 全民健保：一體適用、看病方便且便宜
第二段	說明行銷臺灣特色的方式： ❶ 請國外 YouTuber 體驗文化，藉此行銷臺灣的食物、文化、景點 ❷ 多利用社群媒體分享有關臺灣之美的照片或影片
結論句	全民都應該要徹底地認同與珍惜臺灣，努力讓全世界知道臺灣是一個很棒的國家。

Step 3. 參考範文

As a Taiwanese, I am intensely proud of my country. Once well-known as "the beautiful island," Taiwan is a small country surrounded by sea. However, it has gradually developed many **features** which attract many foreigners to come to visit and stay. The first thing that I take pride in is our night market culture. Although Taiwan is not big, nearly every big city has night markets. These open-air markets provide a wide range of delicious street food, entertainment, and shopping options. Visitors can enjoy eating, playing, and buying here until or past midnight. Second, I take pride in our national health coverage. Taiwan has the leading universal healthcare system. **Residents** with health smart cards can visit any medical care institutions contracted to the national health insurance system with low medical fees. Since patients' medical records are stored on their smart cards, doctors anywhere in Taiwan can check patients' medical history and prescribe medicine through the system. All these two things prove that Taiwan is indeed a modern and convenient country.

In the **era** of the Internet information explosion, the importance of promoting such a fascinating country cannot be overemphasized. First of all, we can regularly invite YouTubers from other countries to experience life in Taiwan. Then these fun clips can be uploaded and posted on our tourism bureau's website to **introduce** and **promote** Taiwanese local cuisine, indigenous cultures, and tourist attractions. In addition, we can take advantage of social media to share pictures, stories, or videos regarding the beauty of Taiwan with people around the world. Above all, every citizen should fully recognize and cherish Taiwan, making every effort to let the whole world know that Taiwan is a great country.

身為臺灣人，我深深地為我的國家感到驕傲。曾經以「美麗島嶼」馳名，臺灣是一個四周環海的小國。然而，它逐漸發展出許多特色吸引許多外國人來拜訪和定居。第一個讓我感到自豪的是我們的夜市文化。雖然臺灣不大，但幾乎每個大城市都有夜市。這些露天市場提供了多樣性的街頭美食、娛樂和購物選擇。遊客們可以在此享用美食、玩樂與購物直到或超過深夜。第二，我感到自豪的是我們的全民健保。臺灣有頂尖一體適用的醫療系統。擁有健保卡的居民可以到有跟健保局合作的醫療機構看診且醫療費用低廉。因為病人的醫療紀錄都存在他們的健保卡，在臺灣任何地方的醫生可藉由系統確認病人的病史與開藥。這兩件事證明了臺灣確實是一個現代又方便的國家。

　　在網路資訊爆炸的時代，行銷這樣一個吸引人的國家的重要性怎麼強調也不為過。首先，我們可以定期邀請國外的 YouTuber 來體驗臺灣的生活。然後這些有趣的片段可以被上傳和張貼在我們觀光局網站用來介紹與行銷臺灣當地美食、在地文化和旅遊景點。此外，我們可利用社群媒體將有關臺灣之美的照片、故事或影片分享給世界各地的人們。最重要的是，每個公民都應該要徹底地認同與珍惜臺灣，努力讓全世界知道臺灣是一個很棒的國家。

Step 4. 寫作攻略

A. 必學好句

1. Once well-known as "the beautiful island," Taiwan is a small country surrounded by sea. 　曾經以「美麗島嶼」馳名，臺灣是一個四周環海的小國。

> ✎ 善用分詞構句 **V-ing (主動) / p.p. (被動) . . . , S + V . . . .** 讓寫作更精簡流暢。

　　生於貧窮的家庭，Ted 沒有上大學。

→ _____

2. The importance of promoting such a fascinating country cannot be overemphasized. 行銷這樣一個吸引人的國家的重要性怎麼強調也不為過。

> ✎ 善用 **The importance of . . . cannot be overemphasized.** 強調「某件事的重要性」。

　　保護環境的重要性怎麼強調也不為過。

→ _____

B. 必學好字

1. **feature** *n.* 特色
Every city or town in Taiwan has its own distinctive **features**.
臺灣的每座城市或小鎮都有它獨特的特色。

2. **resident** *n.* 居民

   Residents of big cities usually complain about air pollution and traffic congestion.
   大城市的居民經常抱怨空氣汙染和交通堵塞。

3. **era** *n.* 時代

   The **era** of corruption and injustice finally came to an end.
   腐敗與不公正的時代終於結束。

4. **introduce** *v.* 介紹

   The tour guide **introduced** the history of the Roman Empire to us.
   導遊向我們介紹羅馬帝國的歷史。

5. **promote** *v.* 行銷

   The company joined the trade fair to **promote** its newest products.
   這間公司參加貿易展覽會行銷它的最新產品。

C. Extended Writing Map

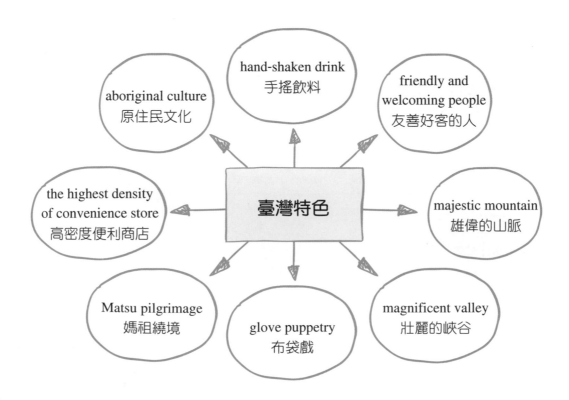

★社區活動三選一

提示：如果你就讀的學校預計辦理一項社區活動，而目前師生初步討論出三個方案：(一) 提供社區老人服務 (如送餐、清掃、陪伴等)；(二) 舉辦特色市集 (如農產、文創、二手商品等)；(三) 舉辦藝文活動 (如展出、表演、比賽等)。這三個方案，你會選擇哪一個？請以此為題，寫一篇英文作文，文長至少 120 個單詞。文分兩段，第一段說明你的選擇及原因，第二段敘述你認為應該要有哪些活動內容，並說明設計理由。 (107 指考)

(一)  (二)

(三)

Step 1. 讀懂題目

閱讀提示說明，理解其問題：

1. 從文字閱讀中找到關鍵字：辦理社區活動三選一
2. 從文本中找到可用的資訊：特色市集 (如農產、文創、二手商品等)
3. 第一段 (說明)：說明你的選擇及原因
4. 第二段 (說明)：敘述活動內容及設計理由
5. 結論：達成社區活動最終目的

 **英文素養寫作攻略**

A. 寫作藍圖

What & Why?　　　　　　　　　　　　　　　　　　What & Why?

Community event

第一段：說明社區活動的選擇及原因

第二段：敘述活動內容與設計理由

choose to organize a fair

❶ performance
❷ bingo game
❸ voluntary donation

❶ convenience
❷ save money
❸ more interaction

forge a relationship of trust and reciprocity

B. 從寫作藍圖持續擴寫

主題句	如果要我從這三種選項挑選其中之一，我會選擇籌劃市集。
第一段	說明社區活動的選擇與原因： ❶ 便利：賣家可推廣產品，買家可以在此一次買許多東西 ❷ 省錢：賣家可省下租金，買家可以優惠價格買到商品 ❸ 更多互動：社區的人會有更多交流，增進對彼此的了解
第二段	敘述活動內容與設計理由： ❶ 表演活動：炒熱歡樂氣氛 ❷ 賓果遊戲：特殊獎品吸引更多人參加 ❸ 捐獻活動：幫助窮人
結論句	我相信這個市集會讓人們走出他們的家，打開心房，並建立信任與互助的關係。

Step 3. 參考範文

    If I were asked to choose among the three options, I would choose to organize a **fair**. At the fair, people in the **community** can sell things, ranging from local agricultural **produce**, cultural creative products to second-hand goods. For one thing, the fair gives sellers an opportunity to showcase and promote their products. Buyers can also purchase a wide range of goods here. For another, it saves sellers' money on renting a store or a booth. As for buyers, there's a good chance that they can enjoy some discounts and get a good bargain because many people in the community are acquaintances. And best of all, through these trading activities, everyone in the community will have more interaction and thus deepen bonds of mutual understanding.

    It would be great if the fair could include some intriguing activities. For example, we could invite students from school bands as well as talented people from the community to give performances, making the event full of joy. What's more, a bingo game could be carried out to attract more people to visit the fair. Those who participate in the fair would have a chance to win the prize. Most important of all, a **voluntary** donation could be held to help the needy. The food, money, or toys received would be dispatched to the orphanages and other charitable organizations, making this event more meaningful. All things considered, I believe this fair would get people out of their homes, open up to each other, and forge a relationship of trust and **reciprocity**.

    如果要我從三種選擇挑選其中之一，我會選擇籌劃一個市集。在這個市集，社區的人們可以出售各種東西，從在地農產品、文創商品到二手商品。一方面，市集給賣家一個機會去展示以及促銷他們的產品。買家在這裡也可以購買許多種類的物品。另一方面，市集可以幫賣家省下租用商店或攤位的錢。至於買家，他們很有可能會因為許多社區的人都是熟人而享有一些折扣，便宜買到東西。最棒的是，透過交易活動，社區裡的每個人將有更多的互動，因而增進對彼此的了解。

    如果市集納入一些吸引人的活動會更好。例如，我們可以邀請學校樂團的學生以及社區有才華的人進行表演，讓活動充滿歡樂。並且，賓果遊戲可被執行吸引更多人來參與活動。參與市集活動的人有機會贏得獎品。最重要的是，可以舉辦自願捐獻活動幫助窮人。收到的食物、錢或玩具會分配給孤兒院和其他慈善機構，使這個活動更有意義。考量到各方面，我相信這個市集會讓人們踏出他們的家，打開心房，並建立信任與互助的關係。

英文素養寫作攻略

Step 4. 寫作攻略

A. 必學好句

1. If I were asked to choose among the three options, I would choose to organize a fair.
如果要我從這三種選項挑選其中之一，我會選擇籌劃市集。

> ✏ 善用 **If + S + V-ed / were . . . , S + would / could / might / should + V. . . .**
> 表達與現在事實相反的假設語氣。

如果要我選慢跑或游泳，我會選擇前者。

→ _____

2. We could invite students from school bands as well as talented people from the community to give performances.
我們可以邀請學校樂團的學生和社區有才華的人來表演。

> ✏ 善用 **A as well as B** 對等片語連接詞，連接對等的單字、片語或子句。若 **as well as** 連接兩個主詞，動詞須依第一個主詞作變化。

這部影片介紹如何搭船去小島，以及你可以去哪裡吃到當地的小吃。

→ _____

B. 必學好字

1. **fair** *n.* 市集
John bought some antique furniture at the **fair**.
John 在市集上買了一些古董家具。

2. **community** *n.* 社區
Betty tells stories to the kids in the local **community** every weekend.
Betty 每個週末都會說故事給當地社區的小孩聽。

3. **produce** *n.* 農產品
With this app, you can order fresh **produce** and have them delivered to your home.
有了這個應用程式，你可以訂新鮮的農產品，並送到你家。

4. **voluntary** *adj.* 自願的；志願的

Ivy and Ken do **voluntary** work for the non-profit organization once a week.

Ivy 和 Ken 每週一次自願為非營利機構服務。

5. **reciprocity** *n.* 互助

Based on the **reciprocity**, we decided to cooperate with ABC company on this development project.

基於互助，我們打算和 ABC 公司合作這個開發計畫。

C. Extended Writing Map

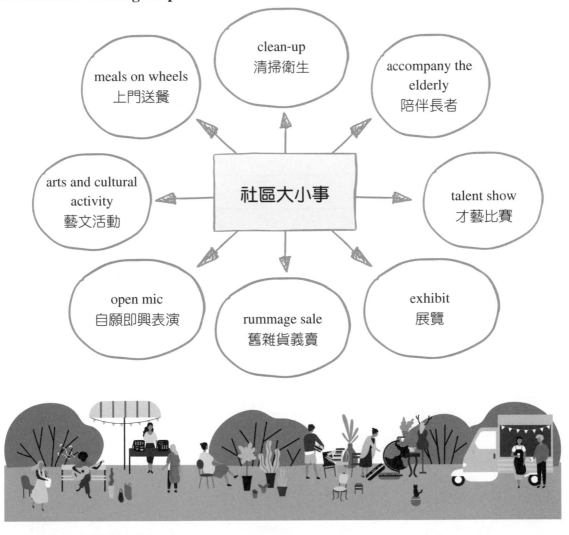

Note

Lesson 6

二十分鐘輕鬆寫作文：實戰演練篇

一、主題寫作

二、圖表寫作

三、看圖寫作

四、信函寫作

英文素養寫作攻略

　　從第四課與第五課，我們了解近幾年考試英文寫作的命題趨勢，題目大多與學生的生活經驗相關，從個人抒發 (106 年指考的寂寞經驗)，擴及家庭 (105 年學測的家事分工)、校園 (109 年指考的校園安全)、社區 (107 年指考的社區活動三選一) 到社會議題 (110 年學測的遊客賞花公德心)，範圍越來越廣，符合課綱所強調的核心素養，學習內容須結合生活情境，與他人及社會有互動。

　　若要避免考試一看到題目腦中一片空白，建議平時除了多方涉獵大量閱讀，也可透過觀察社會脈動、記錄自己平日所見所聞，練習表達看法或抒發感想，從生活累積寫作素材。接下來，我們依序就大考常見的寫作題型：主題寫作、圖表寫作、看圖寫作和信函寫作，來做更進一步的技巧剖析與練習。

一、主題寫作

技巧剖析

　　主題寫作為大考最常見的寫作題型，其文體以第二課所介紹的記敘文、描寫文與說明文為主。面對任一寫作題型，第一件事要讀懂題目，理解問題後再依照提示的要求設定主旨、擬定大綱後下筆。

1. 善用寫作結構

記敘文	運用 5W1H 的方式來描述經驗或事件的過程。
描寫文	使用感官多角度去描繪人物或景物的細節。
說明文	依題幹要求的特定主題和說明方式答題，如逐步列舉、比較對照、討論因果與主題描述。

2. 具體細節鋪陳

　　無論是哪一種文體，落實相關細節的鋪陳，如生動的描述或明確的舉例說明，以及適切的使用轉折用語銜接句子，皆有助於讀者理清邏輯，快速掌握文章重點。

練習一

提示：在資訊爆炸的網路世代，資訊的取得十分容易。然而，網路上的訊息真偽
難辨。你是否有過讀到「假新聞」或收到「假訊息」的經驗？請就這個主
題，寫一篇英文作文，文長約 120 個單詞。文分兩段，第一段說明你認為
假新聞或假訊息會如此氾濫的原因；第二段敘述你或你的親友曾被什麼樣
的報導或訊息誤導過，以及從中得到的啟示。

Step 1. 讀懂題目

閱讀提示說明，理解其問題：

1. 從文字閱讀中找到關鍵字：假新聞、假訊息
2. 從文本中找到可用的資訊：網路訊息真偽難辨
3. 第一段：說明假新聞或假訊息如此氾濫的原因
4. 第二段：敘述被假新聞或假訊息誤導的經驗與啟示
5. 結論：事件的省思

Step 2. 擬定大綱

A. 寫作藍圖

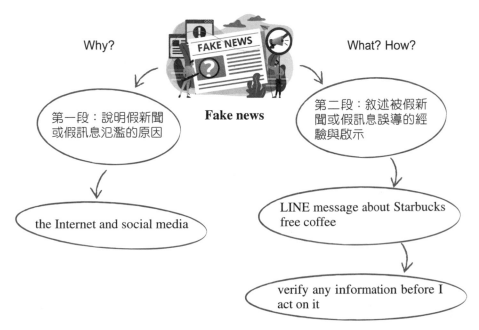

B. 從寫作藍圖持續擴寫

主題句	由於網路使我們生活變得更便利，我們可以全天候發送或接收各式各樣的資訊。
第一段	說明假新聞或假訊息泛濫的原因： ❶ 假新聞大部分來自社群媒體且社群媒體的朋友都是認識的人 ❷ 人們容易被吸引人的標題和聳人聽聞的故事吸引而分享
第二段	敘述被假新聞或假訊息誤導的經驗與啟示： ❶ 社群媒體的星巴克免費訊息 ❷ 行動前要先確認訊息真偽
結論句	在採取行動前查證我收到的任何資訊是重要的。

Step 3. 參考範文

　　With the Internet making our life more convenient, we can send or receive a wide variety of information around the clock. However, it's getting more difficult to distinguish between real and fake news now. In recent years, fake news has become **prevalent** largely due to the social media. Many of our friends on social media are people we trust and know. Accordingly, we are more **inclined** to believe the information or message they shared on it. Moreover, people are more likely to be attracted by catchy headlines and **sensational** stories from the Internet. On seeing such information, a majority of people cannot resist reading and sharing without fact-checking. Worst of all, fake news **spread** like wildfire and badly affect us more than we think.

　　One day morning, I got a LINE message saying that Starbucks would give out free coffee to the first 50 guests. Once I read the message, I rushed to the nearest Starbucks. Surprisingly, no one was waiting in line except for a clerk opening the door. I thought I was the lucky first customer. Soon, I ordered a large latte. Just as I was leaving, the clerk asked me to pay for the coffee. Suddenly it dawned on me that I was tricked by a fake message. Feeling angry and ashamed, I took out my wallet and paid for it. In light of this event, I've learned that it's important to **verify** any information I have been given before acting on it.

> 　　由於網路使我們生活變得更便利，我們可以全天候發送或接收各式各樣的資訊。然而，現在變得越來越難分辨消息的真假。近幾年，假新聞盛行

大部分來自於社群媒體。許多在社群媒體上的朋友是我們信任與認識的人。因此，我們也比較傾向於相信他們分享在上面的資訊或訊息。再者，人們也比較容易被網路上吸引人的標題和聳人聽聞的故事給吸引。一看到這樣的資訊，大多數的人都會沒經過事實查核就忍不住閱讀和分享。更糟的是，假新聞擴散迅速，對我們的影響比想像中的嚴重。

　　有一天早上，我收到一個 LINE 訊息，說星巴克會送給前 50 位客人免費咖啡。我一看到這個訊息，就衝到最近的一間星巴克。令人驚訝的是，除了正在開門的店員外，沒有人在排隊等候。我以為我是第一個幸運的顧客。很快地，我點了一杯大杯拿鐵。就在我要離開時，店員請我付咖啡的錢。我突然意識到我被一則假訊息騙了。感到生氣和慚愧，我拿出錢包付了錢。鑑於這個事件，我了解到在採取行動前查證我收到的任何資訊是重要的。

Step 4. 寫作攻略

A. 必學好句

1. With the Internet making our life more convenient, we can send or receive a wide variety of information around the clock.
   由於網路使我們生活變得更便利，我們可以全天候發送或接收各式各樣的資訊。

   🖊善用 **with + O + OC (V-ing / p.p.)** 來說明原因或表示附帶狀況。

   由於空氣汙染變得更加嚴重，許多居民搬出小鎮。
   → _____

2. Suddenly it dawned on me that I was tricked by a fake message.
   我突然意識到我被一則假訊息騙了。

   🖊善用 **It dawned on sb that . . . .** 表達「某人意識到、開始明白…」。

   Mindy 意識到關於瑜伽自己還有很多要學習的地方。
   → _____

B. 必學好字

1. **prevalent** *adj.* 流行的，普遍的
   Nearsightedness is more **prevalent** among elementary school students.
   近視在國小學童中越來越普遍。

2. **inclined** *adj.* 傾向於…的
   Mark was **inclined** to take this tough job.
   Mark 傾向於接下這份困難的工作。

3. **sensational** *adj.* 聳人聽聞的
   Most **sensational** news stories are written to attract readers' attention.
   大部分聳人聽聞的新聞報導是寫來吸引讀者注意。

4. **spread** *v.* 擴散，散播
   Much to Josh's disappointment, his best friends **spread** rumors about him.
   令 Josh 失望的是，他最好的朋友散播有關他的謠言。

5. **verify** *v.* 查證，證明
   You'd better **verify** the address before sending the report.
   你最好在寄出報告前查證一下地址。

C. 延伸學習

1. bias 偏見	2. half-truth 半真半假的話	3. misinformation 錯誤資訊
4. confirmation 確認	5. media literacy 媒體素養	6. misleading 誤導人的
7. fact-check 事實查核	8. made-up 虛構的	9. reliability 可信度

🎯 練習二

提示：手機遊戲 (mobile game) 推陳出新，讓不少人趨之若鶩。請就這個主題，寫一篇英文作文，文長約 120 個單詞。文分兩段，第一段說明手機遊戲吸引人的原因；第二段則說明過度沉迷手機遊戲會造成的不良影響。

Step 1. 讀懂題目

閱讀提示說明，理解其問題：
1. 從文字閱讀中找到關鍵字：手機遊戲
2. 從文本中找到可用的資訊：推陳出新，讓不少人趨之若鶩
3. 第一段：說明手機遊戲吸引人的原因
4. 第二段：說明過度沉迷手機遊戲會造成的不良影響
5. 結論：過度沉迷手機遊戲所帶來的省思

Step 2. 擬定大綱

A. 寫作藍圖

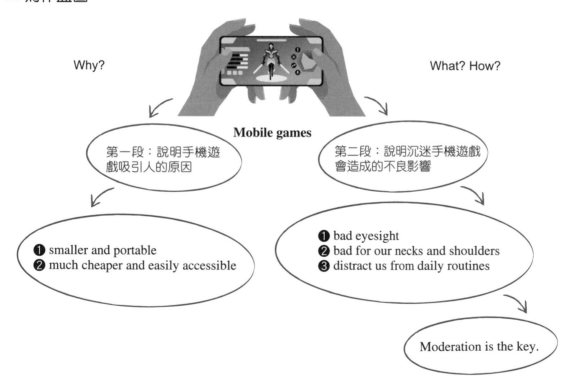

B. 從寫作藍圖持續擴寫

主題句	手機遊戲吸引人不僅是因為我們無論何時何地都可以玩，而且它們也比電視遊樂器便宜。

第一段	說明手機遊戲吸引人的原因： ❶ 可以在相對較小臺且攜帶方便的智慧型手機或平板電腦上玩手機遊戲 ❷ 手機遊戲比起電視遊樂器較便宜且容易取得
第二段	說明過度沉迷手機遊戲造成的不良影響： ❶ 長時間注視螢幕，視力變差 ❷ 總是低頭對肩頸不好 ❸ 在日常生活分心，影響學業或工作任務
結論句	總之，手機遊戲可能是放鬆和消磨時間的好辦法，但我們必須記得適量是關鍵。

Step 3. 參考範文

Mobile games are fascinating not only because we can play them anywhere at any time but also because they are cheaper compared to console games. Unlike traditional console games, mobile games do not require a big device to act as the **platform**. Instead, we can enjoy mobile games on our smartphones or tablets, which are significantly smaller and more **portable**. We only need to reach into our pockets or bags for the phones and then we can start having some fun. Furthermore, mobile games are much cheaper and easily **accessible** than console games. Many of them are either free or at very low prices, and can be downloaded easily. Due to the relatively low barrier to entry, we are more likely to play mobile games and share our gaming experience with others.

Mobile games can be addictive, and spending too much time playing them can have negative effects on our body and life. First, staring for too long at the monitor can **strain** our eyes, leading to bad eyesight. Second, constantly lowering our head is bad for not only our necks but also our shoulders. Third, addiction to mobile games distracts a person from his or her daily routines, such as schoolwork or job tasks. All in all, mobile games may be a good way to relax and kill time, but we need to remember **moderation** is the key.

> 手機遊戲吸引人不僅是因為我們無論何時何地都可以玩，而且它們也比電視遊樂器便宜。不像傳統的電視遊樂器，手機遊戲不需要大設備作為平臺。取而代之地，我們可以在相對較小臺且攜帶方便的智慧型手機或平板電腦上玩。我們只要伸手到口袋或包包拿出手機就可以開始玩得痛快。而且，手機遊戲比起電視遊樂器較便宜且容易取得。許多手機遊戲不是免費就是價

格非常低廉，且下載容易。由於入手門檻較低，我們更有可能去玩手機遊戲，與其他人分享我們的遊戲體驗。

手機遊戲容易使人上癮，而且花太多時間玩它們對我們身體和生活有不好的影響。首先，長時間注視螢幕傷眼，導致視力變差。第二，總是低頭對我們肩頸不好。第三，對手機遊戲成癮會讓人在日常生活分心，例如學業或工作任務。總之，手機遊戲可能是放鬆和消磨時間的好辦法，但我們必須記得適量是關鍵。

Step 4. 寫作攻略

A. 必學好句

1. Mobile games are fascinating not only because we can play them anywhere at any time but also because they are cheaper compared to console games.
   手機遊戲吸引人不僅是因為我們無論何時何地都可以玩，而且它們也比電視遊樂器便宜。

   ✐善用 **not only . . . but also . . .** 表示「不僅…而且…」來連接對等的單字、片語或子句。

   規律的運動不僅能讓幫助我們放鬆，而且改善我們的睡眠品質。
   → _____

2. Many mobile games are either free or at very low prices, and can be downloaded easily.
   許多手機遊戲不是免費就是價格非常低廉，且下載容易。

   ✐善用 **either . . . or . . .** 表示「二擇一」，同樣連接兩個對等的單字、片語或子句。若 **either . . . or . . .** 連接兩個主詞，動詞須依第二個主詞做單複數變化。

   我們可以從商店購買這項產品或是從網路上訂購。
   → _____

B. 必學好字

1. platform *n.* 平臺

As a senior engineer, Sam is quite familiar with many computer **platforms** and operating systems.

身為一個資深工程師，Sam 對於許多電腦平臺和作業系統相當熟悉。

2. portable *adj.* 攜帶方便的

Brian prefers a laptop computer because it is **portable**.

Brian 比較喜歡筆記型電腦因為它攜帶方便。

3. accessible *adj.* 可得到的

Julie made education more **accessible** to students in rural areas by donating books and school supplies.

藉由捐贈書和學校用品，Julie 讓偏鄉的學生接受教育更為容易。

4. strain *v.* 損傷

Listening to loud music for a long time may **strain** your ears.

長時間聽吵雜的音樂可能會損害你的耳朵。

5. moderation *n.* 適度

The doctor advised Helen to drink coffee in **moderation** rather than to excess.

醫生建議 Helen 適度喝咖啡，不要過量。

C. 延伸學習

1. free-to-play 免費遊戲	2. in-app purchase 應用程式內購買
3. aggression 攻擊	4. social isolation 社交孤立
5. sleep problem 睡眠問題	6. listless 無精打采的
7. gaming disorder 電玩失調症	8. obesity 肥胖問題
9. out of control spending 消費失控	10. virtual world 虛擬世界

練習三

提示：打工度假 (working holiday) 在年輕人之間相當流行，尤其是許多大學畢業生會選擇在踏入社會的第一年出國打工度假。請寫一篇英文作文，表達你對這個現象的看法。文長至少 120 個單詞。全文分為兩段，第一段說明出國打工度假的優點為何；第二段則說明出國打工度假須注意的地方。

Step 1. 讀懂題目

閱讀提示說明，理解其問題：

1. 從文字閱讀中找到關鍵字：出國打工度假
2. 從文本中找到可用的資訊：許多大學畢業生會選擇在踏入社會的第一年出國打工度假
3. 第一段：說明出國打工度假的優點
4. 第二段：說明出國打工度假須注意的地方
5. 結論：出國打工度假要做好準備

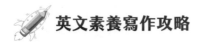

Step 2. 擬定大綱

A. 寫作藍圖

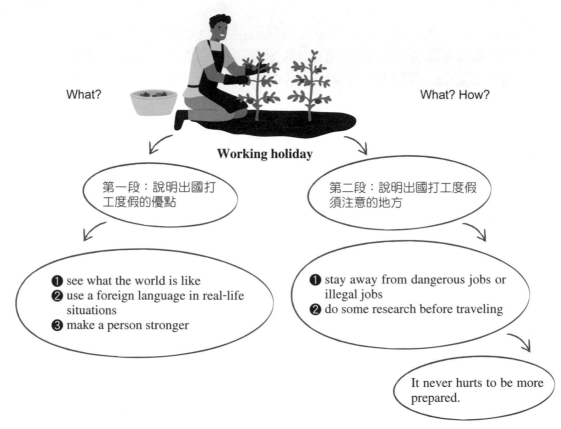

B. 從寫作藍圖持續擴寫

主題句	大學畢業生藉由打工度假去探索世界有增多的趨勢。
第一段	說明出國打工度假的優點： ❶ 有機會從在異國居住和工作看世界 ❷ 有機會在真實情境下使用外語 ❸ 沒有在家來的舒適，在異國生活會使人更堅強
第二段	說明出國打工度假須注意的地方： ❶ 遠離危險或非法的工作 ❷ 去國外旅行前做一些研究 (生活開銷、氣候和居住環境)
結論句	畢竟，做好更多準備沒有壞處。

Step 3. 參考範文

There's an increasing tendency for college graduates to explore the world through working holidays. In my opinion, it is a **once-in-a-lifetime** experience to open their minds to new ideas and perspectives. First of all, working holidays allow young people to have a chance to see what the world is like by living and working in a foreign country. Also, they will get an opportunity to immerse themselves in a different culture and use a foreign language in real-life situations, which helps **boost** their proficiency. Lastly, the experience will definitely make a person more independent because living on foreign **soil** without the comfort of home is a challenge. To sum up, I believe working holidays can broaden one's horizons, improve one's language ability, and help a person mature.

Despite the advantages, people should treat working holidays with **caution**. Numerous unfortunate incidents have happened to young people who go on working holidays. Just like finding any job, people should be careful when choosing what to do. For example, staying away from dangerous jobs or illegal jobs would be the top priority. In addition, they should do some research before traveling to a foreign country. It's important to be **informed** about what life is like there beforehand, such as the cost of living, the climate, and the local laws. After all, it never hurts to be more prepared.

大學畢業生藉由打工度假去探索世界有增多的趨勢。在我看來，打工度假是一個千載難逢的經驗去接受新想法和新觀點。首先，打工度假讓年輕人有機會從在異國居住和工作看世界。而且，他們有機會沉浸在一個不同文化和在真實情境下使用外語，有助於提升語言能力。最後，這個經驗會使一個人更獨立，因為沒有在家來的舒適，在異國生活是一個挑戰。總結來說，我相信打工度假可以開拓視野、改善語言能力及有助於使人變得成熟。

儘管有這些優點，人們對於打工度假應該謹慎。有許多不幸的事件發生在打工度假的年輕人上。就如同找任何工作一樣，人們在選擇要做什麼時應該小心。例如，遠離危險或非法的工作為首要之務。此外，他們應該在去國外旅行前做一些研究。事先知道那裡的生活是怎麼樣的是很重要的，如生活開銷、氣候和當地法律。畢竟，做好更多準備沒有壞處。

Step 4. 寫作攻略

A. 必學好句

1. In my opinion, it is a once-in-a-lifetime experience to open their minds to new ideas and perspectives.
   在我看來，打工度假是一個千載難逢的經驗讓他們接受新想法和新觀點。

   ✎善用 **It + is + Adj. / N + to V . . . .** 為 **it** 當虛主詞的用法，避免主詞太長，句子頭重腳輕。

   與我的家人環遊歐洲是一次難忘的經歷。
   → _____

2. Just like finding any job, people should be careful when choosing what to do.
   就如同找任何工作一樣，人們在選擇要做什麼時應該小心。

   ✎善用 **Just like . . . , S + V . . . .** 表示「就如同…一樣，…」，此時 **like** 為介系詞。

   就如同解謎一樣，你必須找到線索，接著從中推論。
   → _____

B. 必學好字

1. **once-in-a-lifetime** *adj.* 一生中難得一次，千載難逢的
   For Ann, watching the fashion show in Paris is a **once-in-a-lifetime** opportunity.
   對 Ann 來說，在巴黎看時裝秀是一生中難得一次的機會。

2. **boost** *v.* 提升
   Kate tried to **boost** her self-confidence by practicing positive thinking.
   Kate 嘗試藉由練習正向思考提升她的自信心。

3. **soil** *n.* 國家，國土
   It takes a lot of effort for Gary to get used to his life on foreign **soil**.
   Gary 需要付出很多努力才能習慣在異國的生活。

4. **caution** *n.* 謹慎，小心

First and foremost, we should proceed with **caution** when facing a challenge.
首要的是，當我們面對挑戰時應該謹慎行事。

5. **informed** *adj.* 了解情況的

Sammy was asked to keep her supervisor **informed** about the progress of the project.
Sammy 被要求讓她主管了解專案的進度。

C. 延伸學習

1. overseas 在海外 (的)　　　　　2. new friendship 新友誼
3. personal growth 個人成長　　　4. professional skills 專業技能
5. deep exploration 深度探索　　　6. out of comfort zone 離開舒適圈
7. self-sufficient 自給自足的　　　8. culture shock 文化衝擊
9. travel scam 旅遊詐騙　　　　　10. dip a toe in the water 探索新事物

Note

Try it!

Class: _____   *Name:* _____   *No.* _____

提示：全球受疫情影響，許多國家甚至是臺灣的學校都有採取遠距學習 (distance learning)。請寫一篇英文作文，表達你對這個現象的看法。文長至少 120 個單詞。全文分為兩段，第一段說明遠距學習的優點為何；第二段說明你對這種學習方式的看法及原因。

Step 1. 讀懂題目

閱讀提示說明，理解其問題：
1. 從文字閱讀中找到關鍵字：_____
2. 從文本中找到可用的資訊：_____
3. 第一段：_____
4. 第二段：_____
5. 結論：_____

Step 2. 擬定大綱

A. 寫作藍圖

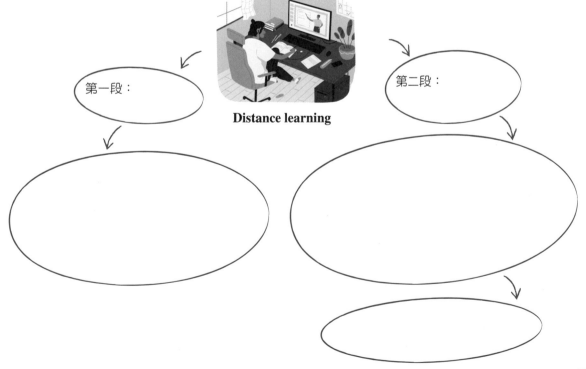

第一段：

Distance learning

第二段：

B. 從寫作藍圖持續擴寫

1. 主題句：＿＿＿＿＿＿＿＿＿＿＿＿＿＿＿＿＿＿＿＿＿＿＿
2. 第一段：＿＿＿＿＿＿＿＿＿＿＿＿＿＿＿＿＿＿＿＿＿＿＿
   ＿＿＿＿＿＿＿＿＿＿＿＿＿＿＿＿＿＿＿＿＿＿＿＿＿＿＿
3. 第二段：＿＿＿＿＿＿＿＿＿＿＿＿＿＿＿＿＿＿＿＿＿＿＿
   ＿＿＿＿＿＿＿＿＿＿＿＿＿＿＿＿＿＿＿＿＿＿＿＿＿＿＿
4. 結論句：＿＿＿＿＿＿＿＿＿＿＿＿＿＿＿＿＿＿＿＿＿＿＿

Step 3. 開始寫作

二、 圖表寫作

技巧剖析

　　圖表寫作的文體通常以說明文為主，內容大多與調查或研究所提供的統計數字或數據分布有關。在第四課中，我們有提及大考常見的圖表類型。

表格	可呈現各項目或類別的總數對比。
長條圖	可比較一個項目在不同時間點的變化或不同項目在同一時間點的數值。
圓餅圖	可描述在整體數據中各種項目的比例。
折線圖	可分析數據隨時間變化的趨勢或分析兩種以上數據隨時間變化的交互作用或影響。

1. 描述圖表重點

　　遇到圖表寫作，除了讀懂題目外，還要懂得分析與解讀圖表，將圖表中的數據及訊息轉換為文字敘述。須注意的是，通常只要依照題幹指定描述的內容，挑選最具代表性的項目，觀察該項目在圖表中的數據或趨勢變化做客觀與重點式描述及比較。建議描述的方式可按總數由高到低 (表格)、時間順序從過去到現在 (長條圖或折線圖)、比例大小由大到小 (圓餅圖)，此處可套用第四課最後一部分關於描述圖表、數據增減趨勢與項目比較的句型。

❶ 依照題幹指定，挑選**最具代表性項目**
❷ 針對該項目數據或趨勢做**重點式描述**

2. 從經驗呼應主題

　　分析圖表後，通常第二段會請你以自身的生活經驗與圖表的狀況比較異同，透過舉例說明或提供理由加以闡述你的看法。切記文章結論須與圖表主題相呼應，以達畫龍點睛之效。

練習一

提示：下圖呈現的是臺灣某間高中學生的平均睡眠時間，請寫一篇至少 120 個單詞的英文作文。文分兩段，第一段描述該圖所呈現的特別現象；第二段請說明你的睡眠狀況，如時間、品質等，並說明其理由。

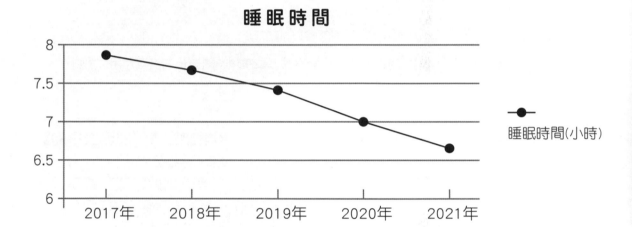

睡眠時間

Step 1. 讀懂題目

閱讀提示說明，理解其問題：
1. 從文字閱讀中找到關鍵字：臺灣某間高中學生的平均睡眠時間
2. 從圖表中找到可用的資訊：睡眠時間 (小時)、2017 年到 2021 年
3. 第一段：描述該圖所呈現的特別現象
4. 第二段：說明你的睡眠狀況，如時間、品質等，並說明其理由
5. 結論：睡眠對生活的影響

Step 2. 擬定大綱

A. 寫作藍圖

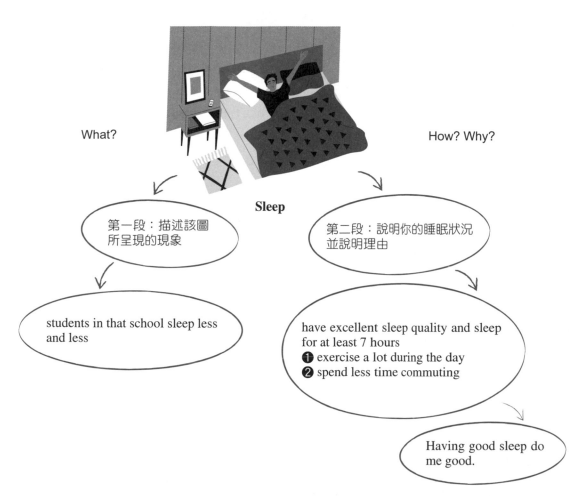

Sleep

What?

第一段：描述該圖所呈現的現象

students in that school sleep less and less

How? Why?

第二段：說明你的睡眠狀況並說明理由

have excellent sleep quality and sleep for at least 7 hours
❶ exercise a lot during the day
❷ spend less time commuting

Having good sleep do me good.

B. 從寫作藍圖持續擴寫

主題句	這張折線圖顯示臺灣一所高中的學生從 2017 年到 2021 年平均的睡眠時數。
第一段	描述該圖的特別現象： ❶ 整體而言，那所學校的學生睡得越來越少 ❷ 在 2021 年，平均一天只睡 6.7 小時，比 2017 年少 1.2 小時
第二段	說明你的睡眠狀況： 睡眠品質好，每天至少睡 7 小時 理由： ❶ 白天運動量大 ❷ 不用早起通勤
結論句	簡而言之，我確信擁有好品質的睡眠對我有好處且讓我第二天精神充沛。

Step 3. 參考範文

The line graph demonstrates the **average** hours of sleep of students from a Taiwan senior high school from 2017 to 2021. Overall, students in that school sleep less and less. Back in 2017, students slept about 7.9 hours on **average**. However, the number continued to decrease as time went by. In 2021, students slept on average only 6.7 hours a day, which were lower than the number in 2017 by 1.2 hours. It appears that the **trend** will continue into the future.

It is well known that having adequate and good quality of sleep is essential for students. My quality of sleep is excellent. Every day, I sleep for at least 7 hours. Sometimes, I sleep in on weekends. Because I always have a long and hard day at school, I tend to get **exhausted** at night. Once I lie in bed, I can fall asleep right away. **Insomnia** has never been an issue for me. The reasons I get such a good night's sleep are probably that I exercise a lot during the day and that I don't spend much time **commuting** to school. The sports I play wear me out, so I don't toss and turn in bed. I live near my school, so I don't need to get up too early for school. In brief, I'm certain that having good quality of sleep would do me good and make me feel energized for the next day.

這張折線圖顯示臺灣一所高中的學生從 2017 年到 2021 年平均的睡眠時數。整體而言，那所學校的學生睡得越來越少。早在 2017 年時，學生平均睡眠時間約為 7.9 個小時。然而，隨著時間推移，數字開始往下降。在 2021 年，學生平均一天只睡 6.7 小時，比 2017 年的數字少 1.2 小時。似乎這種趨勢將持續到未來。

眾所皆知，擁有足夠和良好品質的睡眠對學生來說至關重要。我的睡眠品質絕佳。每天，我至少睡 7 小時。有時，我在週末睡晚一些。因為我總是在學校度過漫長又辛苦的一天，所以晚上往往會筋疲力竭。一旦我躺上床，就可以馬上睡著。失眠對我來說從來不是一個問題。我晚上可以睡個好覺的原因可能是我白天運動量很大，而且我不用花太多時間通勤。運動使我筋疲力盡，所以我不會在床上翻來覆去。我住在學校附近，所以不需要太早起上學。簡而言之，我確信擁有好品質的睡眠對我有好處，且讓我第二天精神充沛。

Step 4. 寫作攻略

A. 必學好句

1. It appears that the trend will continue into the future.
   似乎這種趨勢將持續到未來。

   🖊善用 **It appears that . . . .** 表示「似乎…」。

   似乎這場流行病將對旅遊業造成嚴重衝擊。
   → _____

2. Once I lie in bed, I can fall asleep right away.
   一旦我躺上床，就可以馬上睡著。

   🖊善用 **Once S + V . . . , S + V . . . .** 表示「一旦…，就…」。

   一旦 Jill 下定決心要減肥，她一個月內就能達成目標。
   → _____

B. 必學好字

1. **average** *adj.* 平均的；*n.* 平均
   The **average** age of the contestants for the game is 30.
   這場遊戲參賽者的平均年齡為 30 歲。
   On **average**, Japanese people earn more than Taiwanese people.
   平均而言，日本人比臺灣人賺得錢還多。

2. **trend** *n.* 趨勢
   The figure shows that there has been an upward **trend** in food delivery service in the last two months.
   數字顯示過去兩個月食物外送服務一直呈現上升的趨勢。

3. **exhausted** *adj.* 筋疲力竭的
   Kyle felt **exhausted** after running the marathon.
   Kyle 在跑完馬拉松後感到筋疲力竭的。

4. **insomnia** *n.* 失眠

   Since Natasha suffered from **insomnia**, she had to take sleeping pills to help her get to sleep.

   因為 Natasha 失眠，她需要吃安眠藥幫助她入睡。

5. **commute** *v.* 通勤

   It takes Rita one hour to **commute** from her home to the office every day.

   Rita 每天需花一個小時從她家通勤到辦公室。

C. 延伸學習

1. an early bird 早起的人
2. a night owl 晚睡的人
3. oversleep 睡過頭
4. meditation 冥想
5. fatigue 疲憊
6. lifestyle adjustment 改變生活方式
7. have a nightmare 做惡夢
8. stay up 熬夜
9. sleep like a log 睡得很香
10. wakeful 難以入睡的

練習二

提示：下圖呈現的是臺灣某間高中學生上網時間的分配，請寫一篇至少 120 個單詞的英文作文。文分兩段，第一段描述該圖所呈現的特別現象；第二段請說明整體而言，你在網路上時間的分配與該間高中學生的異同，並說明其理由。

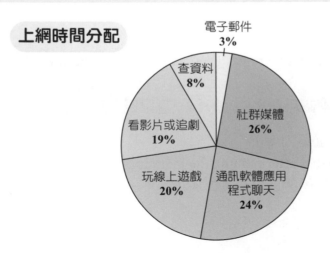

上網時間分配

電子郵件 3%
查資料 8%
社群媒體 26%
看影片或追劇 19%
通訊軟體應用程式聊天 24%
玩線上遊戲 20%

Step 1. 讀懂題目

閱讀提示說明，理解其問題：

1. 從文字閱讀中找到關鍵字：臺灣某間高中學生上網時間的分配
2. 從圖表中找到可用的資訊：上網時間分配
3. 第一段：描述該圖所呈現的特別現象
4. 第二段：說明你在網路上時間的分配與該間高中學生的異同，並說明其理由
5. 結論：網路對生活的影響

Step 2. 擬定大綱

A. 寫作藍圖

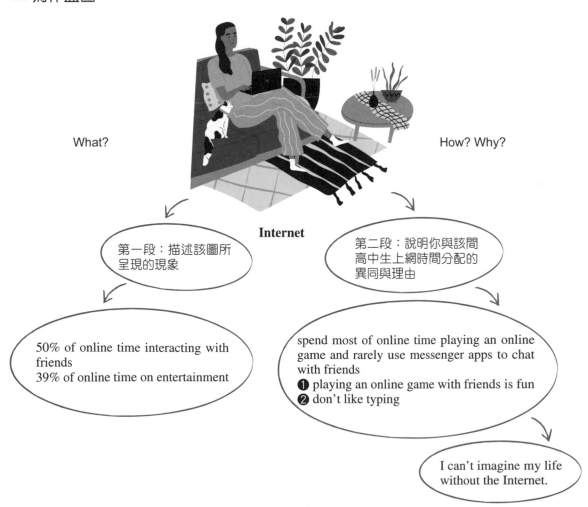

What?

How? Why?

Internet

第一段：描述該圖所呈現的現象

第二段：說明你與該間高中生上網時間分配的異同與理由

50% of online time interacting with friends
39% of online time on entertainment

spend most of online time playing an online game and rarely use messenger apps to chat with friends
❶ playing an online game with friends is fun
❷ don't like typing

I can't imagine my life without the Internet.

B. 從寫作藍圖持續擴寫

主題句	這張圓餅圖說明臺灣某間高中學生的上網時間分配。
第一段	描述特別現象： ❶ 50% 的上網時間花在與朋友交流，39% 的時間花在娛樂活動 ❷ 花較少時間在上網查資料或確認電子郵件
第二段	說明你上網時間分配與圖表的異同： ❶ 花最多上網時間在玩線上遊戲和查遊戲技巧與竅門，偶爾使用社群媒體 ❷ 很少使用通訊軟體應用程式在聊天 理由： ❶ 與朋友一起玩線上遊戲很有趣 ❷ 不喜歡打字，所以很少用通訊軟體應用程式在聊天
結論句	我甚至無法想像我的生活沒有網路。

Step 3. 參考範文

The pie chart illustrates what students from a Taiwanese senior high school do when they connect to the Internet. **Roughly** speaking, they spend 50% of their online time interacting with their friends either by using social media or by chatting through messenger apps. They also spend about 20% of their online time playing games and 19% watching videos or **binge-watching**, both of which are quite relaxing activities. However, they don't spend much time looking up information or checking their email. To them, the Internet is a tool they use to socialize with people and **loosen up**.

The Internet plays a vital role in my life. Unlike those students, I spend most of online time using my smartphone or computer to play an online game. There is nothing more fun than playing an online game with friends. The game I play is very popular among the game players around the world, and a lot of my classmates play it, too. I have to stay connected to the Internet to play the game. By doing so, the system would find worthy **opponents** for me to play with. I have a great time competing with players around the world. In addition, I search for tips and tricks related to the game online to win the game. Like most teenagers, I also use social media to share my life with my friends occasionally. Nevertheless, I rarely use messenger apps to chat with my friends because I don't like typing. Apparently, using the Internet has become an **unstoppable** trend. I can't even imagine my life without it.

　　這張圓餅圖說明臺灣某間高中學生的上網時間分配。大致上，他們把 50% 的上網時間花費在使用社群網站和透過通訊軟體應用程式聊天。他們也花了約 20% 的上網時間玩遊戲及 19% 的時間看影片或追劇，兩者皆是相當放鬆的活動。然而，他們沒有花太多時間在查閱資料或確認電子郵件。對他們而言，網路是用來與人社交與放鬆的工具。

　　網路在我的生活扮演極為重要的角色。不同於那些學生，我花大部分上網時間在使用智慧型手機和電腦玩線上遊戲。沒有什麼比和朋友一起玩線上遊戲來的有趣。我玩的遊戲在全世界的遊戲玩家中很受歡迎，而且有很多同學也在玩。我必須連上網路才能玩遊戲。藉此，系統會幫我找到旗鼓相當的對手和我一起玩。我很開心能與世界各地的玩家競爭。此外，為了在遊戲取勝，我會上網搜尋與遊戲相關的技巧和竅門。如同大部分的年輕人，我偶爾也會使用社群媒體與我的朋友分享生活。然而，我很少使用通訊軟體應用程式跟我朋友聊天因為我不喜歡打字。顯而易見地，使用網路已經變成不可阻擋的趨勢。我甚至無法想像我的生活沒有它。

Step 4. 寫作攻略

A. 必學好句

1. They also spend about 20% of their online time playing games and 19% watching videos or binge-watching, both of which are quite relaxing activities.
他們也花了約 20% 的上網時間玩遊戲及 19% 的時間看影片或追劇，兩者皆是相當放鬆的活動。

✎善用 **S + V . . . , 數量詞 (one / both / some / many . . .) of + 關係代名詞 which** 引導的形容詞子句，特別注意本句後方的關係代名詞為 **which**。

　　Lisa 有許多家用電器，其中一些是日本製的。
→ _____

2. There is nothing more fun than playing an online game with friends.
沒有什麼比和朋友一起玩線上遊戲更有趣。

✎善用 **There is nothing + 形容詞比較級 + than + N / V-ing . . . .** 表示「沒有什麼比…更…的」。

沒有什麼比減少工業排放物更重要的。

→ _____

B. 必學好字

1. **roughly** *adv.* 大致地，粗略地
The price of raw materials has increased **roughly** 20%.
原物料價格上漲約 20%。

2. **binge-watch** *v.* 追劇
I decided to **binge-watch** the entire season of *Friends* this summer vacation.
我決定這個暑假要看完整季的《六人行》。

3. **loosen up** (使) 心情放鬆
Taking a bubble bath helps **loosen** Nancy **up**.
洗泡泡浴幫助 Nancy 心情放鬆。

4. **opponent** *n.* (比賽中的) 對手
Frank was defeated by his **opponent** in a tennis match.
Frank 在網球比賽中被對手擊敗。

5. **unstoppable** *adj.* 不可阻擋的
Owing to the increased use of fossil fuels, global warming has become **unstoppable**.
由於化石燃料使用的增加，全球暖化已變得不可阻擋。

C. 延伸學習

1. stream music 串流音樂
2. check the weather 查詢天氣
3. read news 讀新聞
4. gather information 蒐集資料
5. make a reservation 預約
6. search for directions 尋找方向
7. buy or sell goods 買賣商品
8. pursue interests 追求嗜好
9. online course 線上課程
10. download the software 下載軟體

 **Try it!**

Class: _____ *Name:* _____ *No.* _____

> 提示：下圖呈現的是臺灣某城市不同年段的族群平均每月網路購物消費金額情況
> 的圖表，請寫一篇至少 120 個單詞的英文作文。文分兩段，第一段描述該
> 圖表呈現之現象；第二段描述你或家人的購物習慣及你對此現象的看法。

Step 1. 讀懂題目

閱讀提示說明，理解其問題：

1. 從文字閱讀中找到關鍵字：

_____

_____

2. 從文本中找到可用的資訊：_____

3. 第一段：_____

4. 第二段：_____

5. 結論：_____

某城市市民平均每月網路購物消費金額

（圖表：縱軸 0 至 3000 元，橫軸 15–29歲、30–49歲、50歲以上，分 2011年、2016年、2021年三組）

Step 2. 擬定大綱

A. 寫作藍圖

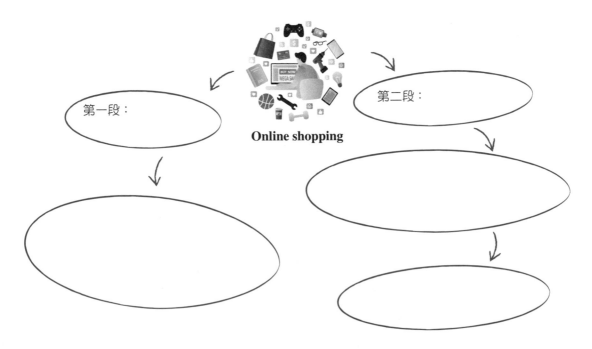

第一段：

Online shopping

第二段：

B. 從寫作藍圖持續擴寫

1. 主題句：_____

2. 第一段：_____
   _____

3. 第二段：_____
   _____

4. 結論句：_____

Step 3. 開始寫作

三、 看圖寫作

技巧剖析

　　常見的看圖寫作有 A. 連環圖與 B. 照片寫作。

　　A. 連環圖的題目通常會提供 3 到 4 張漫畫圖，須依序或自訂圖片順序，將圖片中的情境串聯成一個故事，有時候第 4 張圖是問號圖，須依據前 3 張圖發想一個合理的結局，其文體通常以記敘文為主。

　　B. 照片寫作題目通常會提供 1 到 2 張照片圖，第一段描述照片中的人、事、物、場景或事件；第二段則是敘述接下來的結果或者以某人的立場發表看法。因此，通常第一段為描寫文，第二段為記敘文或說明文。

1. 起承轉合與加臺詞

　　看圖寫作若要拿高分，除了須遵守提示的需求，也考驗你看圖說故事的編劇能力──運用觀察力描述人事物及發揮想像力營造故事的「起承轉合」，豐富文章內容。

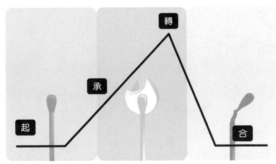

起	故事的開頭，通常會初步描述角色的外觀、行為與所處的場景，目的在於設定情境框架，帶出故事後續發展。
承	承接上述內容，提供更詳細的說明，慢慢帶入事件的核心。
轉	事件的高潮或意外轉折點，通常是角色遭遇到問題或麻煩。
合	故事的結局。

　　為了讓故事描述更為生動，除了使用修飾語 (如形容詞、副詞、片語、子句等)，也可適時穿插一到兩句直接引述句，替角色加臺詞，使故事更生動。此類

型寫作通常是描述過去發生的事件，時態使用過去式。相較於連環圖，單張照片寫作少了許多線索，因此所需要的想像空間更大。遇到此題目時，切勿心急平鋪直敘，單就描述照片內容就結束。而是要先確認照片的重點，即你所要訴說故事的主題，才能將圖片中的內容表達更具體、更精確。例如，觀察人物時，可先從其相貌與穿著定義其身分，接著再往前推想該人物行為背後可能的原因，往後推想該人物行為可能造成的後果。以此步驟為基礎，開始進行想像，必要時可把自己與照片有關的經歷或感受作連結，讓文章更生動。

2. 注意連貫性與結局

　　由於故事通常會依照時間順序或因果關係發展，妥善運用時間副詞與轉折用語為故事開頭、串聯情節、帶入轉折、畫下結局能讓整個故事發展更有連貫性，閱讀起來更為流暢。此處可參考第二課記敘文的時間鋪陳與第三課第二部分轉折用語的魔法。這裡的結局技巧主要是針對記敘文的結局，通常一個事件的結尾會帶給人影響或啟發，故此處可參考第二課記敘文的四種常見寫法 —— 感想、期望、啟示、勉勵。

練習一

提示：請仔細觀察以下三幅連環圖片的內容，並想像第四幅圖片可能的發展，然後寫出一篇文長至少 120 個單詞，涵蓋每張圖片內容且結局完整的故事。

Step 1. 讀懂題目

閱讀提示說明，理解其問題：
1. 從文字閱讀中找到關鍵字：觀察三幅連環圖片的內容，想像第四幅圖片可能的
　　　　　　　　　　　　　　發展
2. 從圖片中找到可用的資訊：veterinarian (獸醫)
3. 第一段：依序描述連環圖片內容 (起 + 承)
4. 第二段：提供一個完整的結局 (轉 + 合)
5. 結論：流浪狗不再流浪

Step 2. 擬定大綱

A. 寫作藍圖

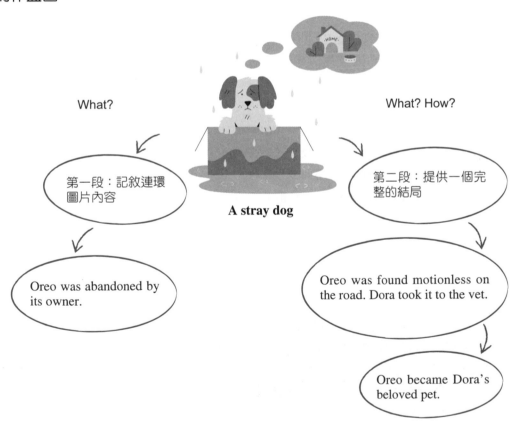

What?

What? How?

A stray dog

第一段：記敘連環
圖片內容

第二段：提供一個完
整的結局

Oreo was abandoned by
its owner.

Oreo was found motionless on
the road. Dora took it to the vet.

Oreo became Dora's
beloved pet.

B. 從寫作藍圖持續擴寫

主題句	有一天，一隻小狗被主人拋棄遺留在垃圾桶旁的紙箱內。
第一段	起：小狗第一次被主人拋棄成為流浪狗 承：為了活下去必須與其他流浪狗爭搶食物
第二段	轉：小狗被 Dora 發現在路邊一動也不動，Dora 將牠帶去看獸醫 合：小狗復原，Dora 決定養牠
結論句	小狗不再是一隻可憐的流浪狗，而是 Dora 最愛的寵物。

Step 3. 參考範文

One day, a puppy named Oreo was **abandoned** by its owner and left in a paper box near a trash can. It was the first time that Oreo had been left alone on the roadside, and it didn't understand why its owner had done this to it. From that day on, poor Oreo became a **stray** dog. It had to look for food in the garbage dump, like all the other stray dogs. It turned out that these stray dogs had to fight over food and eat people's **leftovers**.

It was hard, however, for the stray dogs to survive. The next day, near the garbage dump, a girl named Dora found Oreo motionless on the road. Without hesitation, she immediately took Oreo to the vet. Luckily, Oreo wasn't seriously hurt. "It fainted from hunger. With good care, I believe it would recover in a week." the vet said. On hearing it, Dora felt relieved and decided to take Oreo home. Dora took good care of Oreo and it seemed to like her. Dora was happy to see Oreo **recover** and decided to keep it. Now, they often play together in the yard happily. Oreo is no longer a poor stray dog but rather Dora's **beloved** pet.

有一天，一隻名為 Oreo 的小狗被主人拋棄遺留在垃圾桶旁的紙箱內。這是 Oreo 第一次被單獨遺留在路邊，牠不知道為什麼主人會這樣對待牠。從那天起，可憐的 Oreo 便成了流浪狗。如同其他流浪狗，牠必須在垃圾堆裡找食物。結果是這些流浪狗必須爭搶食物，吃人們的剩飯剩菜。

然而，對於這些流浪狗來說要活下去不容易。隔天，在垃圾堆旁，一位名為 Dora 的女孩發現 Oreo 在路邊一動也不動。毫不遲疑，她馬上帶 Oreo 去看獸醫。幸運的是，Oreo 沒有嚴重受傷。獸醫說：「牠因為飢餓而昏倒了。我相信只要細心照料一個禮拜內牠可以復原。」Dora 一聽，鬆了一口氣

並決定把 Oreo 帶回家。Dora 細心照顧 Oreo，而 Oreo 好像喜歡她。Dora 很開心看到 Oreo 復原，決定要養牠。現在他們時常在庭院玩得很開心。Oreo 不再是一隻可憐的流浪狗，而是 Dora 深愛的寵物。

Step 4. 寫作攻略

A. 必學好句

1. It turned out that these stray dogs had to fight over food and eat people's leftovers.
   結果是這些流浪狗必須爭搶食物，吃人們的廚餘。

   🖊善用 **It turned out that . . . .** 表示「結果是…」。

   結果 Becky 昨晚就發高燒了。
   → _____

2. Oreo is no longer a poor stray dog but rather Dora's beloved pet.
   Oreo 不再是一隻可憐的流浪狗，而是 Dora 最愛的寵物。

   🖊善用 **. . . no longer . . . but rather . . . .** 表示「…不再是…而是…」。

   這間房間不再是我的遊戲室，而是 Alice 的書房。
   → _____

B. 必學好字

1. **abandon** *v.* 遺棄，拋棄
   Michael **abandoned** his truck in the mountains because it broke down.
   Michael 把他的卡車遺棄在山區因為它故障了。

2. **stray** *adj.* 流浪的；走失的
   Jennifer launched a campaign to encourage the adoption of **stray** cats.
   Jennifer 發起一項鼓勵認養流浪貓的活動。

3. **leftover** *n.* 剩飯剩菜
   Leo takes the **leftovers** home if he can't finish his meal at a restaurant.
   若 Leo 沒在餐廳吃完，他會把剩飯剩菜打包回家。

4. **recover** *v.* 完全恢復健康

Peter was not allowed to leave the hospital until he **recovered** from the operation.

直到自手術完全恢復健康前，Peter 不被允許離開醫院。

5. **beloved** *adj.* 深愛的

Bella was very sad because her **beloved** boyfriend passed away.

Bella 非常難過，因為她深愛的男朋友去世了。

C. 延伸學習

1. street dogs 流浪犬	2. animal shelter 動物收容所
3. rescue center 救護中心	4. starving 快餓死的
5. communicable 傳染性的	6. rehome 為 (寵物) 找個新家
7. vaccinate 給…接種疫苗	8. rabies 狂犬病
9. infection 感染	10. microchipped 植入晶片的

 **Try it!**

Class: _____ *Name:* _____ *No.* _____

> 提示：下圖為某活動的新聞畫面，你認為他們的訴求是什麼？你對這個活動有什麼想法？請根據此圖片寫一篇英文作文，文長約 120 個單詞。文分兩段，第一段描述圖片的內容，包括其中的人及其舉牌訴求；第二段則表達你對這個活動的看法。

Step 1. 讀懂題目

閱讀提示說明，理解其問題：

1. 從文字閱讀中找到關鍵字：

_____

2. 從文本中找到可用的資訊：

_____

3. 第一段：_____

4. 第二段：_____

5. 結論：_____

Step 2. 擬定大綱

A. 寫作藍圖

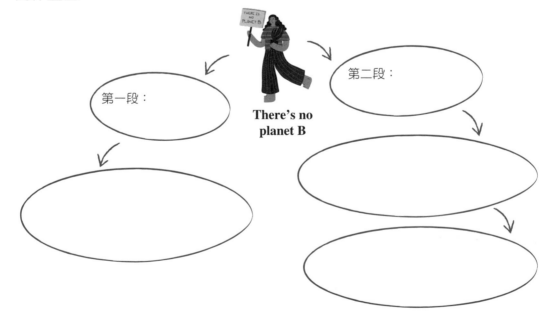

There's no planet B

第一段：

第二段：

B. 從寫作藍圖持續擴寫

1. 主題句：_____

2. 第一段：_____
   _____

3. 第二段：_____
   _____

4. 結論句：_____

Step 3. 開始寫作

四、信函寫作

技巧剖析

信函寫作可分為商業信件與一般信件，而以往大考的信函寫作以一般信件為主。同樣地，下筆前要讀懂提示，依提示內的指定情境，確認對象姓名 (收件人稱謂與你的署名)，說明來信目的。由於信函寫作內容多為描述當時的情況及想法，時態使用以現在式為主。若談論已經發生的事件或過往的經驗則使用過去式。

1. 目的要明確

常見信函寫作目的有：向對方提出訴求 (請願信)、邀請對方參與活動 (邀請函)、給與對方建議或勸告等。一般開頭建議使用簡單明確的句子表明來信目的，不宜使用過於冗長或複雜的句型。若通信對象為長輩或熟人，或內容為表達致歉或感謝，可在開頭加入一至兩句問候語，避免過於直接。

2. 格式要用對

常見信件格式有兩種，一種是齊頭式 (商業信件)，另一種是半齊頭式 (一般信件)。齊頭式的書寫一律向左對齊，段落之間要空行，結尾敬語需與正文間空一行；半齊頭式的日期、結尾敬語和簽名置中對齊，收件人稱謂向左對齊，每段開頭要空格。

齊頭式　　　　　　　　半齊頭式

❶ 日期　❷ 稱謂　❸ 正文　❹ 結尾敬語　❺ 簽名

英文素養寫作攻略

常見的結尾敬語可分為正式與非正式用法，請見下表：

正式	Respectfully (yours)、Sincerely (yours)、Yours truly, 等。
非正式	Regards、Cheers、Yours、Best wishes, 等。

練習一

提示：你很久沒聯絡的朋友最近因為比賽落敗情緒低落。你 (英文名字必須為 Alan 或 Ashley) 打算寫一封信鼓勵對方 (英文名字必須假設為 Noah 或 Mia)，並提供對方一些方法來重振精神，擺脫沮喪，文長至少 120 個單詞。

Step 1. 讀懂題目

閱讀提示說明，理解其問題：
1. 從文字閱讀中找到關鍵字：很久沒聯絡的朋友因為比賽落敗情緒低落
2. 從文本中找到可用的資訊：建議對方一些方法來重振精神，擺脫沮喪
3. 第一段：表明來信目的
4. 第二段：提出解決方法
5. 結論：鼓勵朋友擺脫沮喪

Step 2. 擬定大綱

A. 寫作藍圖

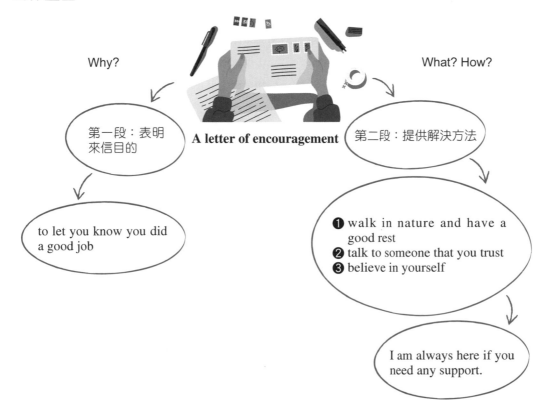

Why?

第一段：表明
來信目的

to let you know you did
a good job

A letter of encouragement

What? How?

第二段：提供解決方法

❶ walk in nature and have a
good rest
❷ talk to someone that you trust
❸ believe in yourself

I am always here if you
need any support.

B. 從寫作藍圖持續擴寫

主題句	我寫這封信是為了跟你說你已經表現很棒了。
第一段	表明來信目的 (鼓勵對方)： ❶ 雖然沒贏得決賽，但確實盡全力挑戰自己 ❷ 你進步神速讓許多人感到驚訝，包括我 ❸ 不要讓負面情緒阻擋你追求目標
第二段	提供解決方法： ❶ 走入大自然好好休息 ❷ 和一個信任的人談談 ❸ 相信你自己
結論句	若你需要任何支持我永遠在這裡。

Step 3. 參考範文

January 10, 20XX

Dear Noah,

How have you been? It has been more than two years since we graduated from junior high school. Recently, I read your social media post and knew that you have been a little bit down in the dumps. I am writing this letter to let you know you already did a good job. Although you didn't win the final, you did make every effort to challenge yourself. To be honest, your hard work and rapid **progress** also surprised many people, including me. Keep in mind that never let negative voices inside your head get in the way of **pursuing** your goal.

The following are some tips that I can give you to help you feel better. First, take a walk in nature and have a good rest. You can take a trip to the mountains or the seaside where you can totally relax yourself and distract attention from **gloomy** thoughts. Then, talk to someone that you trust rather than bottle your feelings up. Once you get it off your chest, you will feel a sense of relief. All you need to do is believe in yourself! You have amazing potential. Don't let failure hold you back from **fulfilling** your dream. You will eventually overcome the sadness and **regain** confidence. I am always here if you need any support.

Yours,

Ashley

20XX 年 1 月 10 日

親愛的 Noah：

　　近來好嗎？自從國中畢業後我們有超過兩年沒見面了。最近，我讀了你在社群媒體上的貼文，得知你一直情緒低落。我寫這封信是為了跟你說你已經表現很棒了。雖然你沒贏得決賽，但你確實盡全力挑戰自己。老實說，你的努力與進步神速也讓許多人感到驚訝，包括我。請記住不要讓你腦中負面的聲音阻擋你追求目標。

　　以下是我給你的一些訣竅希望能幫助你感覺好一些。首先，走入大自然好好休息。你可以去山區或是海邊旅行，在那裡你可以完全放鬆自己，分散對沮喪想法的注意力。再者，和一個信任的人談談，不要壓抑你的感受。一旦你把你的感受一吐為快，你會感到如釋重負。你所需要做的就是相信你自

己！你擁有非常好的潛力。不要讓失敗阻礙你實現夢想。你最終將會克服悲傷和重拾信心。若你需要任何支持我永遠在這裡。

你的好友，

Ashley

Step 4. 寫作攻略

A. 必學好句

1. I am writing this letter to let you know you already did a good job.
   我寫這封信是為了跟你說你已經表現很棒了。

   > 🖊善用 **I am writing this letter to + V . . . .** 表達寫信目的。

   我寫這封信是要對你的幫忙表示感激。

   → _____

2. You can take a trip to the mountains or the seaside where you can totally relax yourself and distract attention from gloomy thoughts.
   你可以去山區或是海邊旅行，在那裡你可以完全放鬆自己，分散對沮喪想法的注意力。

   > 🖊善用 **. . . N + where + S + V . . . .**，此句為關係副詞 **where** (表示地方) 引導子句修飾前面的先行詞。

   我們喜歡可以品嘗特色食物和觀賞魔術秀的餐廳。

   → _____

B. 必學好字

1. **progress** *n.* 進步
   Under the professor's guidance, Karen has made some **progress** in playing the cello.
   在教授的指導下，Karen 在演奏大提琴已有些進步。

2. **pursue** *v.* 追求
   Linda quit her job and decided to **pursue** her goal of becoming a YouTuber.
   Linda 辭掉工作，決定追求當 YouTuber 的目標。

3. **gloomy** *adj.* 沮喪的，消沉的

After breaking up with his girlfriend, Jason became very **gloomy**.

與女友分手後，Jason 變得非常沮喪。

4. **fulfill** *v.* 實現

Visiting Mayan ruins has **fulfilled** Zack's childhood dreams.

參觀馬雅遺跡已實現 Zack 的童年夢想。

5. **regain** *v.* 重新獲得，恢復

Sophia **regained** consciousness after being treated for a month in the hospital.

Sophia 在醫院治療一個月後恢復意識。

C. 延伸學習

1. discouraged 洩氣的	2. surrender 投降
3. burden 負擔	4. strength 優點，強項
5. talented 有天賦的	6. faith 信心
7. lift sb's spirits 使某人提振精神	8. open up to sb 對某人傾吐心聲
9. beat yourself up 過分苛求自己	10. back sb up 支持某人

Try it!

Class: _____ *Name:* _____ *No.* _____

提示：你 (英文名字必須為 Morris Wang 或 Karen Chen) 在班上或社團被指派一項
任務，必須邀請一位校外人士 (可以是社會名人、YouTuber 或專家等) 四
月底來學校演講，請在信中大致描述此次邀請對方演講的目的及你希望對
方演講的主題與內容。

Step 1. 讀懂題目

閱讀提示說明，理解其問題：

1. 從文字閱讀中找到關鍵字：_____

2. 從文本中找到可用的資訊：_____

3. 第一段：_____

4. 第二段：_____

5. 結論：_____

Step 2. 擬定大綱

A. 寫作藍圖

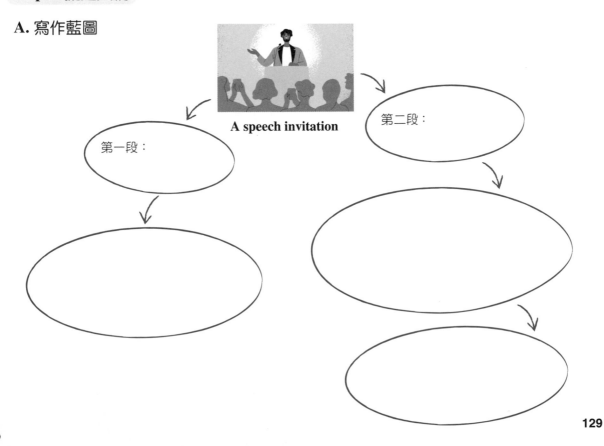

A speech invitation

第一段：

第二段：

B. 從寫作藍圖持續擴寫

1. 主題句：_____

2. 第一段：_____

   _____

3. 第二段：_____

   _____

4. 結論句：_____

Step 3. 開始寫作

Note

Note

神拿滿級分——英文學測總複習

孫至娟　編著

- 重點搭配練習：雙效合一有感複習，讓你應試力 UP ！

- 議題式心智圖：補充時事議題單字，讓你單字力 UP ！

- 文章主題多元：符合學測多元取材，讓你閱讀力 UP ！

- 混合題最素養：多樣混合題型訓練，讓你理解力 UP ！

- 獨立作文頁面：作答空間超好運用，讓你寫作力 UP ！

- 詳盡解析考點：見題拆題精闢解析，讓你解題力 UP ！

大考翻譯 實戰題本

王隆興 編著

1. 全新編排五大主題架構，串聯三十回三百句練習，爆量刷題練手感。
2. 融入時事及新課綱議題，取材多元豐富又生活化，命題趨勢一把抓。
3. 彙整大考熱門翻譯句型，提供建議寫法參考字詞，循序漸進好容易。
4. 解析本收錄單字補充包，有效擴增翻譯寫作用字，翻譯技能點到滿。

國家圖書館出版品預行編目資料

英文素養寫作攻略／郭慧敏編著.――初版一刷.――
臺北市：三民，2022
面；　公分.――（英語Make Me High系列）

ISBN 978–957–14–7381–9　（平裝）
1. 英語 2. 寫作法

805.17　　　　　　　　　　111000563

英語 *Make Me High* 系列

英文素養寫作攻略

編 著 者	郭慧敏
責任編輯	楊雅雯
美術編輯	黃霖珍
內頁繪圖	高宗源

發 行 人	劉振強
出 版 者	三民書局股份有限公司
地　　址	臺北市復興北路 386 號 (復北門市) 臺北市重慶南路一段 61 號 (重南門市)
電　　話	(02)25006600
網　　址	三民網路書店 https://www.sanmin.com.tw

出版日期	初版一刷 2022 年 3 月
書籍編號	S871590
I S B N	978-957-14-7381-9

三民書局

英語 *Make Me High* 系列

英文素養
寫作攻略 解析本

郭慧敏 編著

專為 **108** 課綱
量身打造的英文素養寫作寶典

1 解構大考素養情境寫作命題，
快速掌握寫作心法。

2 從審題構思到組織寫作架構，
逐步培養寫作實力。

3 提供大考各類寫作題型攻略，
全面提升寫作能力。

三民書局

Contents

英文素養寫作攻略 解析本

Lesson 1

(無標準解答，可讓學生自由分享。)

Lesson 2

一、記敘文

1. (E) 2. (A) 3. (F) 4. (C) 5. (D) 6. (B)

二、描寫文

1. The final exam week is a nightmare for Sam. He has been bombarded with tests and assignments from six classes.
2. Your words are like a sharp knife cutting my heart into millions of pieces.
3. During holidays, I enjoy taking a walk into the woods, listening to the natural symphony played by the birds, frogs, and insects.

三、說明文

(無標準解答，可讓學生自由分享。)

Lesson 3

一、2 個寫作三角：構思三角、表達三角

1. The most important things for coping with depression are to seek help from someone you trust and get treatment from mental health professionals.
2. Getting along with friends and family not only makes you feel relieved but also stops you dwelling on negative thoughts.
3. Getting a diagnosis from doctors can help you recognize the symptom early and get well soon.
4. Doing these two things can assist you come out of depression faster.

二、轉折用語的魔法

1. 順序
1. (D) 2. (B) 3. (A) 4. (C)

2. 因果
1. (C) 2. (D) 3. (B) 4. (A)

3. 比較與對比

1. (C)　2. (A)　3. (B)　4. (D)

4. 舉例、補充與強調

1. (D)　2. (B)　3. (C)　4. (A)

Lesson 4

1. As；far；as

2. since / because

3. One；Another

4. With

5. bar；provides / gives

6. In；conclusion

Lesson 5

一、個人抒發

寂寞經驗

1. Not until four p.m. did Carol finish her homework.
2. Hotpot is to winter as ice cream is to summer.

二、家庭議題

家事分工

1. Instead of staying at home, Peter always goes hiking on the weekend.
2. Peggy made resolutions to motivate herself to perform better such as studying harder, exercising more, and saving more money.

三、社會觀察

賣場週年慶

1. When the police arrived at the bank, the two robbers had escaped / run away.
2. Giving up piano is the last thing Sam would do.

排隊現象

1. It is unlikely for Joanne not to find a job after graduation.
2. Why not leave the sofa and go out for a walk?

高學歷找工作

1. Because of heavy rain, we have no choice but to cancel the outdoor activities.
2. As the saying goes, "Look before you leap."

四、創意發想

行銷臺灣

1. Born into a poor family, Ted didn't go to college.
2. The importance of protecting the environment cannot be overemphasized.

社區活動三選一

1. If I were asked to choose jogging or swimming, I would choose the former.
2. The video shows how to take a ship to the island as well as where you can eat local snacks.

Lesson 6

一、主題寫作

練習一

1. With the air pollution getting more serious, many residents move out of the small town.
2. It dawned on Mindy that she still had so much to learn about yoga.

練習二

1. Regular exercise can not only help us relax but also improve our sleep quality.
2. We can either buy this product in stores or order it online.

練習三

1. It is an unforgettable experience to travel around Europe with my family.
2. Just like solving puzzles, you need to find clues and then make inferences from them.

Try it!

提示：全球受疫情影響，許多國家甚至是臺灣的學校都有採取遠距學習 (distance learning)。請寫一篇英文作文，表達你對這個現象的看法。文長至少 120 個單詞。全文分為兩段，第一段說明遠距學習的優點為何；第二段說明你對這種學習方式的看法及原因。

閱讀提示說明，理解其問題：
1. 從文字閱讀中找到關鍵字：遠距學習
2. 從文本中找到可用的資訊：全球受疫情影響，許多國家甚至是臺灣的學校都有採取遠距學習
3. 第一段：說明遠距學習的優點
4. 第二段：說明你對這種學習方式的看法及原因
5. 結論：遠距學習的省思

A. 寫作藍圖

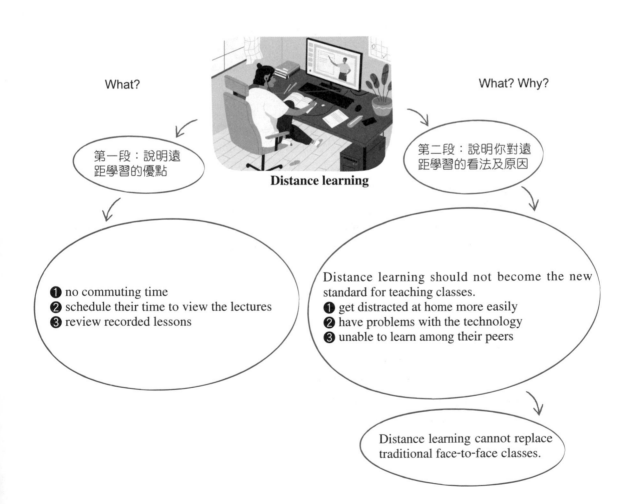

What?

第一段：說明遠距學習的優點

Distance learning

What? Why?

第二段：說明你對遠距學習的看法及原因

❶ no commuting time
❷ schedule their time to view the lectures
❸ review recorded lessons

Distance learning should not become the new standard for teaching classes.
❶ get distracted at home more easily
❷ have problems with the technology
❸ unable to learn among their peers

Distance learning cannot replace traditional face-to-face classes.

B. 從寫作藍圖持續擴寫

主題句	自從 COVID-19 大流行以來世界發生許多變化，其中一個發生巨大變化的領域是教育。
第一段	說明遠距學習的優點： ❶ 不需花費通勤的時間 ❷ 可以自己安排時間觀看課程 ❸ 可以複習已經錄製的課程或重複觀看不好理解的部分課程
第二段	說明你對遠距學習的看法： 遠距學習不應該成為課堂教學新標準。 原因： ❶ 學生在家上課容易分心 ❷ 技術問題 (如上網速度慢) ❸ 無法親自和同儕們一起學習
結論句	遠距學習無法取代傳統面對面課堂教學模式。

Step 3. 開始寫作

A lot of changes have taken place in the world since the COVID-19 pandemic hit, and one area that changed drastically was education. Students could not go to school, but the Internet provided a solution, with video conferencing software such as Google Meet. This allowed students to participate in what is known as "distance learning," so they could stay safe from the deadly virus. The teacher would teach the class as normal, and in some ways, this was a good thing. For example, no time was spent getting to and from school for anyone involved. Moreover, for classes that were lectures, students could often schedule their own time to view it. They could also review recorded lessons or go over parts of the lessons that were hard to understand. Thanks to distance learning, students are given more control over their studies.

While there certainly are advantages to distance learning, I don't think it should become the new standard for teaching classes. To begin with, students can get distracted at home more easily than in a classroom. Some without self-discipline are even more likely to put off the assignment or skip class. In addition, different students might have problems with the technology, such as slow Internet connections. Most important, though, is that students are unable to learn among their peers in person. I believe a lot of learning comes from such classroom interaction. Thus, distance learning cannot replace traditional face-to-face classes.

二、圖表寫作

練習一

1. It appears that the pandemic will severely impact the travel industry.
2. Once Jill makes up her mind to lose weight, she can achieve the goal in one month.

練習二

1. Lisa has <u>many</u> / <u>a lot of</u> domestic appliances, some of which are made in Japan.
2. There is nothing more important than reducing industrial emissions.

Try it!

提示：下圖呈現的是臺灣某城市不同年段的族群平均每月網路購物消費金額情況
的圖表，請寫一篇至少 120 個單詞的英文作文。文分兩段，第一段描述該
圖表呈現之現象；第二段描述你或家人的購物習慣及你對此現象的看法。

某城市市民平均每月網路購物消費金額

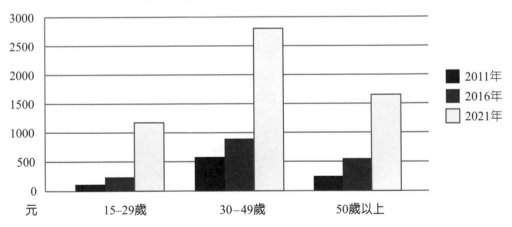

Step 1. 讀懂題目

閱讀提示說明，理解其問題：

1. 從文字閱讀中找到關鍵字：臺灣某城市不同年段的族群平均每月網路購物消費
金額情況的圖表
2. 從圖表中找到可用的資訊：2011、2016、2021 年、15–29 歲、30–49 歲、50 歲
以上
3. 第一段：描述該圖表呈現之現象
4. 第二段：描述你或家人的購物習慣及你對此現象的看法
5. 結論：網路購物對生活的影響

Step 2. 擬定大綱

A. 寫作藍圖

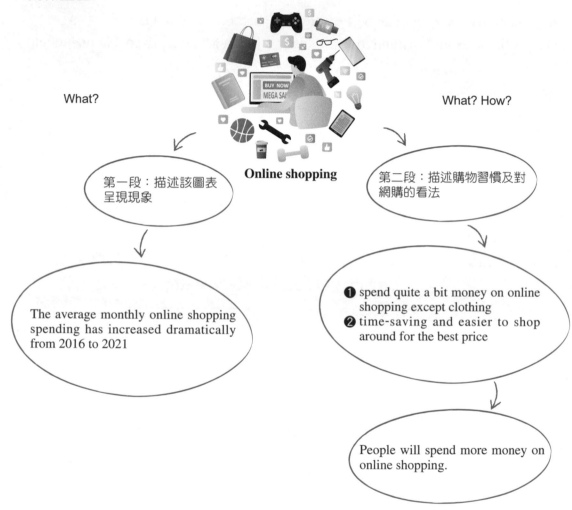

Online shopping

What?

第一段：描述該圖表呈現現象

The average monthly online shopping spending has increased dramatically from 2016 to 2021

What? How?

第二段：描述購物習慣及對網購的看法

❶ spend quite a bit money on online shopping except clothing
❷ time-saving and easier to shop around for the best price

People will spend more money on online shopping.

B. 從寫作藍圖持續擴寫

主題句	此長條圖顯示 2011 年、2016 年和 2021 年臺灣某城市三個不同年齡族群的平均每月網路購物支出。
第一段	描述該圖表呈現的現象： ❶ 2011 年 30–49 歲族群花得最多，15–29 歲族群花最少。 ❷ 2016 年，三個族群每月網購消費金額都提高。 ❸ 2016 年到 2021 年，三個族群每月網購消費金額急遽上升。

第二段	描述你或家人的購物習慣及你對網購的看法： ❶ 網購省時、好比價，全家都是網購狂熱者。 ❷ 因為免運和價格優惠，父母習慣上網買家電和廚具用品。 ❸ 除了衣服想要親自試穿外，物品幾乎都在網路上買。
結論句	毫無疑問地，由於網路購物有那麼多好處，人們很有可能將會花更多錢在此。

Step 3. 開始寫作

The bar chart shows three different age groups' average monthly expenditure on online shopping in a city in Taiwan in 2011, 2016, and 2021. In 2011, people aged between 30 to 49 spent an average monthly amount of money that was a little over NT$500, and that group was spending the most among the three groups. The age group between 15 to 29 spent the least each month, whereas those over 50 years old spent about NT$250 per month. And for all three of these groups, the average monthly online shopping spending increased in 2016. However, the average monthly online shopping spending for all three groups has increased dramatically from 2016 to 2021. Among them, the 30 to 49 age group still has the most spending power. It is likely that this trend will continue in the years to come.

Online shopping has caught on in recent years, and it is also changing the way we shop. Buying online saves us a lot of time as we don't have to walk to a physical store. In addition, it's easier to shop around for the best price because all of it can be done on the Internet. Honestly speaking, my family and I are enthusiastic online shoppers. We spend quite a bit of money doing online shopping for almost everything except clothing. For instance, my brother and I often order food and groceries online by using food delivery apps. As for my parents, they get used to purchasing household appliances and cooking supplies online due to free shipping and special discounts. Only with clothes do we still want to try them on before buying them. Undoubtedly, there's a strong possibility that people will spend more money on online shopping with so many adavantages of it.

三、看圖寫作

練習一

1. It turned out that Becky had a high fever last night.
2. This room is no longer my playroom but rather Alice's study.

Try it!

提示：下圖為某活動的新聞畫面，你認為他們的訴求是什麼？你對這個活動有什麼想法？請根據此圖片寫一篇英文作文，文長約 120 個單詞。文分兩段，第一段描述圖片的內容，包括其中的人及其舉牌訴求；第二段則表達你對這個活動的看法。

Step 1. 讀懂題目

閱讀提示說明，理解其問題：

1. 從文字閱讀中找到關鍵字：某活動新聞畫面、舉牌訴求
2. 從圖片中找到可用的資訊：There is no planet B. Save the Earth.
3. 第一段：描述圖片內容，包括其中的人及其舉牌訴求
4. 第二段：表達你對這個活動的看法
5. 結論：對活動的省思

Step 2. 擬定大綱

A. 寫作藍圖

What?

What? How?

There's no planet B

第一段：描述圖片內容

第二段：表達你對活動的看法

❶ one family holds up signs
❷ there's no planet B

agree with the idea the family puts forward

I would join this family and hold up a sign in support of this green campaign.

B. 從寫作藍圖持續擴寫

主題句	人類對於我們稱為家的地球已經造成了許多破壞。
第一段	描述圖片內容： ❶ 這家人是環保主義者 ❷ 柔性舉牌告訴人們「地球只有一個」的這個事實
第二段	表達對活動的看法： 身為一個高中生，我同意這家人所提出保護地球的想法 ❶ 如果我們一直破壞地球，所有生物都會受害 ❷ 若越來越多人如同這家人這麼愛護地球，我們所在的世界會更乾淨、安全和健康 ❸ 每個人都應該盡力讓我們唯一的地球更適合居住
結論句	如果有機會，我樂意加入這家庭，並舉牌響應這個環保運動。

Step 3. 開始寫作

Human beings have caused a lot of damage to this planet we call home. Because of this fact, many people feel that it is vitally important to get the word out so that people become more aware of this problem. One way this is done is through forms of protest. For example, some protestors take to the streets to stop a large company from polluting the air or the water. Other methods take a gentler approach such as the family in the picture. They could all be described as environmentalists, which means they care about the environment and want it to be healthy. The signs that the family members are holding tell the truth that all people should think about. By saying "there is no planet B," it lets people know that we only have one planet. If we destroy this one, there is no other planet to go to.

As a senior high school student, I agree with the idea this family puts forward—save the Earth. Just like the family's signs say, we have no other options than to live here on Earth. If we continue to kill our planet, all living things will suffer. I believe if more people cared for the Earth as much as this family does, we'd have a cleaner, safer, and healthier world to live in. Everyone must do his or her part to make the only one planet we have more livable. If given the chance, I would gladly join this family and hold up a sign in support of this green campaign.

四、信函寫作

練習一

1. I am writing this letter to express my gratitude for your help.
2. We like the restaurant where we can taste special food / specialties and watch the magic show.

Try it!

提示：你 (英文名字必須為 Morris Wang 或 Karen Chen) 在班上或社團被指派一項任務，必須邀請一位校外人士 (可以是社會名人、YouTuber 或專家等) 四月底來學校演講，請在信中大致描述此次邀請對方演講的目的及你希望對方演講的主題與內容。

Step 1. 讀懂題目

閱讀提示說明，理解其問題：

1. 從文字閱讀中找到關鍵字：在班上或社團被指派一項任務，邀請一位校外人士四月底來學校演講
2. 從文本中找到可用的資訊：邀請對方演講的目的及希望對方演講的主題與內容
3. 第一段：表明來信目的
4. 第二段：說明希望對方演講的主題與內容
5. 結論：希望對方能盡快回信接受邀請

Step 2. 擬定大綱

A. 寫作藍圖

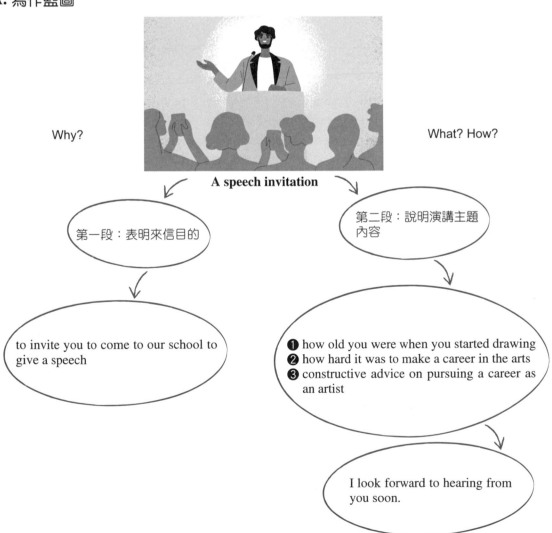

Why?　　　　　　　　　　　　　　　　　What? How?

A speech invitation

第一段：表明來信目的

第二段：說明演講主題內容

to invite you to come to our school to give a speech

❶ how old you were when you started drawing
❷ how hard it was to make a career in the arts
❸ constructive advice on pursuing a career as an artist

I look forward to hearing from you soon.

B. 從寫作藍圖持續擴寫

主題句	我寫這封信是為了詢問您是否有意願來敝校就您的人生和職業作演講。
第一段	來信目的 (邀請對方來學校演講)： ❶ 介紹自己 (從小就是您的漫畫迷，喜歡您出色的畫畫技巧及所創作的那些絕妙故事) ❷ 表明邀請原因 (漫畫社社員，想知道您為何選擇想當漫畫家)
第二段	演講主題和內容： ❶ 從幾歲開始畫畫 ❷ 從事這份行業的甘苦談 ❸ 給未來想從事這行業的我們一些建設性建議
結論句	我希望能早日收到您的來信。

Step 3. 開始寫作

January 21, 20XX

Dear Mr. Chang,

I'm a student at San Min High School, and I have been a fan of your comic books since I learned how to read. I think you have incredible illustration skills, and I love those marvelous stories you create. Once I begin reading one of your comic books, I can't put it down until I've finished it! Many of my classmates and I are members of the manga club, and we are very interested in learning about how you chose your career as a comic book writer and illustrator. For this reason, I am writing this letter to inquire if you would be willing to come to our school to give a speech about your life and career.

We would like you to be our guest speaker because your thoughts would enable us to gain insights into our future. We are eager to learn about how old you were when you started drawing, and how hard it was to make a career in the arts. Also, we need your constructive advice on pursuing a career in this field. The speech is scheduled for April 30, from 2 p.m. to 3 p.m. We are in desperate need of a speaker like you to share your experience with us. Please let me know whether you would be interested in speaking. Thank you in advance and I look forward to hearing from you soon.

Sincerely,

Morris Wang

20 稱霸 分鐘 大考英文作文

王靖賢　編著

- 共16回作文練習，涵蓋大考作文3大題型：看圖寫作、主題寫作、信函寫作。根據近年大考趨勢精心出題，題型多元且擬真度高。
- 每回作文練習皆有為考生精選的英文名言佳句，增強考生備考戰力。
- 附方便攜帶的解析本，針對每回作文題目提供寫作架構圖，讓寫作脈絡一目了然，並提供範文、寫作要點、寫作撇步及好用詞彙，一本在手即可增強英文作文能力。

實用英文文法(完整版) 二版
Practical English Grammar

馬洵、劉紅英、郭立穎 編著
龔慧懿 編審

專為英語學習者編寫的實用文法書

1. 提供完整詳盡的文法說明,說明深入淺出,上課、自學兩相宜。

2. 以表格條列文法重點,搭配情境例句解說,快速理解文法概念。

3. 書末提供文法專有名詞與中英文關鍵字索引,隨時查閱好便利。

4. 可搭配《實用英文文法實戰題本》做更多練習,加強學習效果。

◎封面圖片來源：Shutterstock